Murder in Cleveland, GA

MW00915643

Love Betrayed

If I gaze into thine eyes
Will love look back at me?

If I caress thine face
Will you pull away?
Never wanting my touch again?

If I swear my love for thee
My heart and soul complete,
Will you look away and
Cast that love to the ground at my feet?

I long for thy love,
A gentle whispered kiss, I
Open my heart to let thee see
My love is so complete.

Would thee, could thee, love
Me as much as I love thee,
Or will my uncertain love
Be lost for all eternity?

I cannot look into thine eyes,
Nor swear my love for thee for you my
Dear do not exist except inside of me.

Chapter One

Greg glance his watch and noted the day and time, first Wednesday of June, 2005, one-thirty in the afternoon. In silence, he drove the seven and one half miles outside the city limits of Cleveland, GA., to Crabapple Circle, the scene of the crime. No hurry this time, the bodies removed and the crime scene secured.

He drove slow past the houses and noted this upscale area were unlike many of the subdivisions around White County. The developer chose not to clear the trees in order to shove in as many houses as possible. Instead, tall maple, white pine and oaks dotted the perfectly manicured landscapes.

Multi-colored zinnias and begonias in full bloom overflowed the flowerbeds along with well-tended herbs and lavender blossoms. Tiny pink, red and white rose buds, as faultless as those placed atop a birthday cake by a talented hand, dotted the lush grass somehow making it seem greener.

These were not slapped-together, prefabricated homes but crafted to the owner's specifications; some brick, some stucco but all picture postcard perfect, complete with the Appalachian Mountains as a backdrop. Greg counted ten houses with room for more, but hopped these homeowners wouldn't allow many more anyway. Why ruin perfection?

Rounding a curve, he accelerated for the incline and the huge brick house, the last to be built in the subdivision, loomed in front of him. He pulled his car to the curb and put the Mustang in park then sat and listened to the thrum of its powerful engine for a few moments.

Greg concentrated on the car and pushed the house and the crime to the back of his mind for just a minute.

Remembering when he first bought the junked out heap of faded red metal, a waste of a good machine. He ran his hand over the buttery-soft leather seats and through the windshield admired the candy-apple red paint, hand-rubbed to a deep shine; the four-on-the floor and rebuilt 302 a beautifully restored 1968 Mustang that he'd done himself.

Patience had been key then and the key now. The murders would be brought to justice if only he'd take his time, put things together piece by piece just as he'd done with the car. He turned the key and shut off the engine, breathed in deeply and stepped out into the bright afternoon sunlight.

Hard to believe such a horrendous crime had taken place behind the doors of the beautiful, two-story brick home. Greg ducked under the crime scene tape and moved forward up the cobblestone walk. He took mental notes of the properties exterior.

The same lush lawn and manicured flowerbeds that accented the other homes flowed around this house as well. Four white columns supported the porch roof and distinguished it from the other homes. Large Lion head door-knockers accented the Oak double front doors with bay windows on either side.

Greg made his way around the dried bloody footprints, up on the porch, unlocked the police-installed padlock then entered the expansive foyer. More dried bloody footprints and blood spatters marred the Cherry hardwood floor.

The initial call came in on Saturday. Greg and Chris, his old running buddy from high school, just arrived at the Atlanta Braves game when his pager began to flash 911. By the time he arrived at the scene, Paul Nesbit, the state medical examiner, waited for him just inside the front door. Greg stepped up beside Paul with a clear view into the kitchen, the scene of the crime. His lower jaw dropped and stayed that way until Paul gently pushed it shut again.

The kitchen looked nothing like the large modern room that it was but more like a battlefield. Chairs from the kitchen table overturned, newspaper strewn across the room and paintings ripped from the wall, what a mess. Covering everything was the blood, so thick and heavy that the coppery smell of it made him retch before he got himself under control. My God, he'd never seen so much blood before.

"Jesus Christ Almighty!" he whispered. "What happened?"

Outfitted in surgical garb from head to toe, Paul Nesbit shook his head as he pulled on a pair of surgical gloves. "What a mess, you ready?"

Greg turned to Paul and realized he too needed the protective clothing. "Give me a minute."

He hurried to the State Crime Lab vehicle grabbed a pair of shoe booties, surgical coveralls, hair cover and face mask then snatching up a pair of surgical gloves he hightailed it back toward the house.

From of the corner of his eye, he noticed a small crowd gathered to one side of the lawn, included with them was several newscasters. How do these people hear about this stuff so fast? It's like they have built-in gore antenna or something. He shook his head in disgust, nodded his thanks at the uniformed officers who kept the group at bay and reentered the house.

Paul knelt beside the male victim and looked up as Greg joined him. "I've been doing this for thirty years and I still don't understand how people can do this stuff to each other."

"You okay?" Greg asked.

Paul swiped the back of his hand across his forehead to wipe away the sweat and nodded. "It's been a while since I've seen anything this bad, but I'll be okay once I start working."

Greg returned the nod and pulled a notepad and pen and knelt beside the older man ready to take notes and offer whatever assistance he could.

Paul stared at him for a silent moment he'd been Greg's friend and teacher for a long time so he knew how difficult this case might be for him. "I know nothing like this has happened around here for a long time at least ten years so you haven't had the chance to sink your teeth into a crime scene like this," another silent nod from Greg as he listened.

"Greg, take your time and tell me what you see. Remember what I taught you? The crime scene and the bodies can tell you what happened if you look at them carefully enough. Allow the bodies to tell the story."

Greg rose, looked around for a moment, and then moved over to the breakfast nook, "two cups of coffee on the table." He bent closer, to inhale just a hint of an aroma. The stuff was old and cold. "I'd say they weren't expecting company this morning.

"Someone disarmed the burglar alarm to get the morning paper. I can see from here that the system is off and the newspaper is strewn across the floor and table as if they'd been interrupted at their reading. No signs of a struggle odd."

He stepped closer to the woman's body and pointed. "This wasn't a robbery. Take a look at those rings on her fingers."

Paul nodded his agreement, "so far, so good. What else do you see?"

Greg closed his eyes for a moment, took a deep breath and let it out with an audible sigh before continuing. "The male victim has a shattered leg. You can see the bone protruding through the pant leg. He must have been standing when the first bullet hit him in the right leg."

He knelt close to the body to examine the front of a nearby cabinet. "There's a bullet embedded in this door."

He turned to Paul's assistant, who had quietly entered the room to watch the two men work. "Put a marker here, would you? And get some pictures before the bullet is removed." Satisfied with the other man's nod, Greg stepped away to continue his analysis of the scene.

"The victim was also shot in the right shoulder. From the smell in here he must have been shot in his stomach, which ruptured his bowels." His words seemed to intensify the smell and he shook his head to clear it away. "God, that stinks. Another shot to the head shattered the skull; bone barely attached and dangling." Finished, he turned back to Paul, who nodded in encouragement.

"No more gun shots." Greg finished.

Paul crossed the room to kneel by the body and made a circular motion with his gloved hand. "Tell me what you see here, around the chest area? How about here, around the pelvic area? Tell me, what do you see?"

Greg looked at the front of the dead man's shirt, trying to avoid the unblinking stare of the cold, lifeless eyes and the accusation of that wide-open, contorted mouth.

"There appears to be a slit in the shirt as well as in the pants. What did that?"

The two men stepped out of the way of the photographer. "Always look for the unexpected, Greg. Those slits were made with a knife. Expect to see stab wounds when we undress him."

Greg turned quickly to the man beside him. "Stab wounds? You mean someone shot and stabbed him?"

Again, Paul pointed to the entry wounds. "I know it's hard to tell the difference, but do you see the amount of blood loss from the shoulder and the leg? Now, look at the slits in the shirt and pants. This man was already dead when someone stabbed him repeatedly."

"Why? To make sure he was dead?"

Paul looked at Greg and then back down at the victim. "Because blowing his head off wasn't going to kill him, right?" He shook his head in disbelief. "I don't envy you your job."

Greg jotted down some notes: Male victim—mid fifties. Body slumped on the floor with left leg twisted awkwardly underneath. Shattered bone protruding through pant leg, most probable the fatal wound was either to the stomach or head. Coroner's report will verify conclusions.

Greg placed the notepad in his back pocket and turned his full attention to the female victim. She appeared to be in her mid to late forties. Pink nail polish on her manicured fingernails was partial covered with blood and the right shoulder was blown open; noticeable bone fragments were embedded into the exposed flesh of her upper body. The victim's face and hair were drenched with blood and the wound to the left shoulder seemed identical to that of the right.

A single shot to the lower abdomen ruptured the bladder; the body reeked of stale urine in much the same way the males stank of fecal matter. The shot to the right side of the head had torn away a good portion of the skull and brain tissue oozed and puddle on the floor.

Blood splatter clearly marked the spot where she stood when the first shot entered her body. Still more blood and flesh was splattered across the front of the cabinets, the microwave oven, the wall, and the floor. The splatters on the wall and the oven were high and almost in a straight angle; the other spatters were lower, but had hit in somewhat of an upward spiral, which meant she must have been shot once while standing and the other three times after she fell—probably dying or dead before being stabbed again and again.

"What about shoe prints?" Greg asked. "Whoever did this had to step into the blood to stab them."

"Too smeared," replied Paul.

"Premeditated? But why shoot and stab them?"

"To make a statement? I don't know. I'm just the coroner. You're the detective. You figure it out," Paul responded as he turned the dead man's head.

"How long have they been dead?" Greg asked, and tried not to watch what Paul was doing to the dead man.

"Let's see. It's almost two in the afternoon, and judging by the rigor mortis, I'd say since seven or eight o'clock this morning. That would make the deaths several hours old. Of course, the air conditioner is turned down really low so that could slow down the rigor."

"Were they shot at close range?" Greg asked as he jotted down what Paul said.

Finished with his task, Paul stood, motioned for his assistant to come forward with the camera, and pointed to the areas he wanted photographed. Then he turned back to Greg.

"I can tell you more once I get them to the morgue. A lot of this stuff will have to go to the state crime lab. Their so backed up it could be months before we get the results back" He watched as a team of technicians entered the room and got to work placing markers adjacent to each spent shell, taking

pictures, placing the shells into crime lab
bags, and then tagging each one carefully.

"Who called 911?"

Paul motioned Greg to join him on
the other side of the room so the technicians
could finish with the victims. "One of the
neighbors. Man! What a mess."

Paul glanced around the room and
into the foyer at the massive staircase. "This
guy must have made some serious money to
afford a house like this."

He turned back toward the
technicians. "Get some wide-angle photos of
the victims together."

Greg stepped onto the tarp covering
the hall floor, stripped off his gloves, lab
coat, and shoe covers, and then walked
outside to talk to the neighbors.

Chapter Two

Seeing an officer he recognized, he nods in his direction. "Hi, Sprayberry,"

The tall, lanky, dark-haired officer returns the greeting, "Lieutenant."

"Do you know who called 911?" Greg asks as he wrote the question down in his notepad.

"Sure. I asked them to wait over in their yard. They're over there under the big Maple."

"I see them, thanks." Greg steps off the curb and heads in the direction of the small group of onlookers gathered around the tree, on his approach, he notices the crowd of reporters and cameramen had doubled since he'd gone inside the house. There were also several rather well dressed people who he assumed must be neighbors of the dead couple—income bracket does not define ghouls, he thought in disgust. These people should leave the dead in peace, go home and mind their own business.

When he drew abreast of the neighbors, all conversation stopped. "Good afternoon, folks. I'm Lieutenant Greg Garrison." Pulling his wallet from the back pocket of his jeans, he flips it open to reveal the badge and departmental identification within, "one of you placed the call to 911?"

A blonde petite woman holding a small boy tightly in her arms steps forward. The man at her side reaches for the child and after a moment's hesitation, she hands the child over to him. Pink cheeks streaked with runnels of makeup and blue eyes swollen from too many tears, she responds with a simple, "I did."

"Can you tell me what you saw and heard?"

She shook her head. "Nothing, we got up around eight-thirty this morning, ate breakfast, did a little housework, and then came outside around ten-thirty. My husband and I had just started planting flowers when

Brenda came running out of the house covered with blood—though I didn't know what it was at first. I'd never seen anything like it before.

"The screams were terrifying. We dropped everything and started running toward her. She collapsed at the edge of the lawn before we could get to her." She points in the direction of where Brenda had fallen.

At this point, her husband steps forward. Tall and muscular, he puts his free arm around his wife's shoulders to pull her closer before continuing the story where she left off. "We kept running. I got to her first. There was so much blood. It was all over her—in her hair, on her face, her clothes were covered with the stuff . . ." Staring across the manicured lawns as if he could still see the woman lying there, he shuddered.

"My wife was screaming and crying— the noise brought out the neighbors from across the street and they also rushed over. Brenda opened her eyes and started crying, 'Help them. Please help them.'

"John, he's the neighbor from across the street, and I went inside the house while my wife called 911. My God what a mess we found inside that house."

"Yes, sir I know, I've seen it. What's your name?" Greg asks.

"Frank Coleman. And this is my wife, Joyce."

Another couple steps forward. "My name is Mark Baker" he held out a hand and Greg shook it. "This is my wife, Elaine. I'm the neighbor who went inside with Frank."

Greg wrote the names in his note pad, and then looks from one couple to the other. "You didn't know anything was wrong until the girl came outside? You didn't hear any gunshots or any screams coming from the house?"

Silently the women shake their heads while the men respond, "No" in unison.

"How well did you know these

people?" Greg asks.

Mark Baker, short, stocky, blonde and blue-eyed was the first to answer. "We've only lived in our house for a few months. The subdivision is only a few years old so that might give you an idea of how well any of us know one another.

"I've spoken with him a few times, but never to his wife, who seemed to be a homemaker. He was a doctor. The daughter, Brenda, is a student at the University of Georgia. I've only seen her once before today. She wasn't home too often.

"Can you tell me their names?" Greg asked.

Elaine Baker, desperate to participate in the conversation, spoke up quickly. "Yes Joseph and Bette Armstrong."

"And none of you heard anything?" He stares at them one at a time, waiting for their responses.

Frank Coleman glares back, and looks at his wife and neighbors before answering. "We already answered that question. The first time we realized there was anything wrong was when Brenda came screaming out of the house."

"Mrs. Coleman, you said you and your husband were outside planting flowers. Did you see anyone enter or exit the house before Brenda came out?

She shakes her head. "No. I just saw Brenda."

The little boy squirmed in his father's arms, wanting down—to run and play. Who cared what all these big people had to say when there were so many interesting things to explore in the yard? Frank places him on the ground and watches as he toddles across the lawn.

"Lieutenant, we moved here from the city to get away from crime." He waves a hand in the direction of the Armstrong's house. "I thought this was a peaceful and safe place to raise a family. I guess not. Two people were murdered right next door to us–

–apparently in broad daylight."

Greg moves a little closer, "Cleveland is a very safe place to raise your family, sir. This is only the second recorded homicide in the history of White County. The first was ten years ago. A man murdered his wife and her lover, and then took his own life. So put your mind at ease. You made a good choice."

Hearing a commotion behind him, Greg turns to see the covered bodies of the victims being wheeled from the house on gurneys—cameras flash and the reporter's shouts questions that no one seemed to feel inclined to answer.

"Thanks for your help." He pulls a business card from the pocket of his shirt, handing it to Frank. "If any of you think of anything else give me a call. I'll be in touch if I have any more questions."

"We'll do anything to help," Frank replies.

Greg crosses the lawn and stops next to Paul, who was packing up his gear. "Where'd they take the daughter?"

"White County responded so my guess would be Northeast Georgia Medical Center—that's where they usually go."

"Thanks, Paul for everything." Returning to his car, he calls dispatch to confirm the girl's location, and then leaves the crime scene. He glances at his watch as he pulls away from the curb. The hospital was in Gainesville, about thirty-five miles away so he should get there around eight-thirty or so. This is turning into a long day, he thought—a long, long day.

Chapter Three

As usual, the emergency room was crammed. There were people who'd had colds for days who suddenly decided they needed immediate care along with the real emergencies—cuts requiring stitches, broken bones and possible heart attacks. He'd seen it all before.

Introducing himself to the charge nurse at the sign-in desk, she directed him to "Follow the blue line to the end of the hallway and take a left. Dr. Conner is in the lounge—first room on the right."

Greg found him without a problem. "Dr. Conner, I'm Lieutenant Greg Garrison with the White County Police. I'm working a homicide in Cleveland and our only witness, Brenda Armstrong was brought in here by ambulance this morning. Can you tell me how she's doing?"

Conner, in his late fifties, around six feet tall with a full beard and baldhead, looked tired. No, the man looked like he was about to pass out on his feet, but Greg knew the man would simply keep working—like it or not, that's what emergency room doctors did.

Gathering a stack of charts, notebooks, and pens, Conner asked Greg to walk with him as he checked on patients. He responded readily to Greg's questions. "Sure. I remember her. Two knife wounds to her back—very superficial. Physically, she'll be fine. Mentally; however, I'm not so sure. I've called in a psychiatrist, Dr. Henry Hargrove who's the best we have in this area."

Greg stepped back against the wall or be trampled by a team of doctors and nurses rushing past him with a patient badly bleeding on a gurney. As soon as they were gone, he turned back to the doctor. "When can I talk to her?"

"That's something you'll have to take up with Dr. Hargrove. His orders were very specific. No one is to speak with her. He plans to transfer her to Hall Sanitarium. Have you heard of it?" Greg shook his head to indicate he hadn't. "It's a private sanitarium and I agree wholeheartedly with Hargrove's decision." He shrugged. "Besides, she hasn't spoken since she was brought in so I doubt it would do any good to talk to her."

"Can I at least see her? I promise I won't ask her anything."

"I'm not sure what good you think that will do, but it couldn't cause any damage simply to look at her. We're still waiting for transfer." He glanced at his watch and shook his head in disgust. "It's been hours and hours since we called, but . . . "

Motioning for Greg to follow, he strode down the corridor, pushed open the door of a trauma room, and pointed. "Here she is."

Greg entered the room and stood silently beside the bed for long moments. Even though her chestnut curls were still matted with dried blood, the sleeping woman, who had drawn herself up tightly into a fetal position, was beautiful.

Greg felt anger for the helpless woman––there was no reason she couldn't be clean and comfortable even though she couldn't ask for assistance herself. "Can't someone at least wash her hair?"

"It should have been done hours ago. I'll get a nurse in here immediately."

"Thank you. And you said she hasn't spoken a word since the paramedics brought her in?"

"Nothing, well not anything audible, she's been just like she is now for most of the day." He motioned for Greg to follow him from the room, which he did, though rather reluctantly.

Exiting, they almost collided with two other men who were on their way in to transfer the patient to the sanitarium. The doctor took the time to apologize profusely for her unkempt hair. "I don't know why it was overlooked," he explained. "I am very sorry." The attendants assured him that it wasn't the first time a disheveled patient was transferred and promised that things would be seen to as soon as the transfer was complete. "Good men," he said before starting down the hallway once more.

"How well do you know this Dr. Hargrove?" Greg asked.

"Hargrove is the best in his field. If anyone can help this young lady, he can. But don't take my word for it. Wait a few days, and then go out there to see for yourself. Here," scribbling quickly on a sheet of paper, he tore it from the pad and handed it to Greg. "Here's his phone number. Now I really must get back to work."

"Sure. Thanks for your time."

By the time Greg took the elevator down to the morgue in the hospital's basement it was well after nine o'clock— much closer to nine-thirty really, and he was beginning
to feel the affects of the long, hard day. When the elevator door opened, Paul stepped in.

"Are you leaving? What about the autopsy?"

"Good evening to you too, Greg, yes, I'm leaving. It's late and I'm too tired to start an autopsy tonight. Besides, they're not going anywhere."

"I was hoping to get a head start on this." As soon as the words were out of his mouth, Greg had an urge to kick himself for sounding so much like a whiny brat.

Paul pushed the button for the main floor and waited silently until the elevator doors closed with a soft whoosh. "I'm not keeping you from your investigation. But, I have no intentions of starting an autopsy tonight. Whatever I'd find tonight will be there tomorrow." The elevator doors opened and he stepped into the lobby with Greg following closely on his heals. "Good night, Greg."

"I'm sorry, Paul."

"I know you're anxious to find out what happened. It's quite all right." They left the building together, wishing each other a goodnight as they went their separate ways at the entrance to the parking garage.

*****

Arriving back at headquarters after ten, the front desk clerk stops him. "Garrison, you have a visitor. She's waiting for you over there." He points to a row of chairs.

Greg turns a curious eye in the woman's direction before asking, "Who is she?"

"Don't know, didn't give a name just said she worked for the man who was murdered today. Insisted on talking to the detective in charge, that would be you, Garrison," he finishes then turns back to the well-worn paperback propped open on the counter.

The woman was dressed casually—an Atlanta Braves tee shirt, jeans, and white tennis shoes. Her red hair pulled back into a ponytail. She appeared to be in her late forties and definitely did not seem to be the type who would appreciate anyone saying anything about her was cute, although Greg thought she was exactly that, cute.

At Greg's approach, she stood, around five feet five and of medium build, a noticeable scar on her upper lip pulled her mouth down at the corner, giving her a slightly off-balance, interesting look.

"I'm Lieutenant Garrison. You're waiting to see me?"

"Yes, I'm Beatrice Langston. I'm . . . I was Dr. Armstrong's office manager."

"Let's go in here so we can have some privacy." Greg escorts her to one of the interrogation rooms. "Would you like a cup of coffee? I can't guarantee how fresh it will be though." She shakes her head. "Something else, like a Coke perhaps?" She shakes her head again. After closing the door, he indicates where she should take a seat and he did the same.

"Do you have any ideas about who

would do this to your boss?"

This time she shakes her head so emphatically Greg was fascinated, watching the red ponytail swing wildly from side to side. "No. He was such a kind man. He worked very hard."

"What kind of doctor was he?" Greg asks, flipping open his note pad.

"A plastic surgeon."

Greg jerks his head up to look at her. "Really? Where's his office?"

She had placed her purse too close to the edge of the table, it tottered and she avoided his penetrating gaze busing repositioning it. "1101 Parker Street Do you know where that is?"

Greg sat back in his chair, studying the woman. "Isn't Cleveland a bit out of the way for a plastic surgeon? White County doesn't have a hospital—patients would have to drive all the way to the medical center in Gainesville to have procedures done. Why would he have his office here?"

Still avoiding his gaze, she responds with a shrug of her slender shoulders. "He said he didn't like big cities. He liked the country atmosphere of Cleveland."

Sensing that things were a little off-kilter here—she was definitely hiding something, Greg presses on. "How long has he been here?"

She fidgeted a bit with the strap of her purse, and then unconsciously ran a hand back and forth across her upper lip. "A little over ten years, I went to work for him when he first opened his office."

Greg watches her for a moment, sat forward quickly and asks. "Miss Langston, why are you here? Do you have some information for me—can you help the investigation in any way?"

She glances at him and then quickly away. "No, I don't know anything. I just want to know who you think might have done such a horrible thing." She gets to her feet and heads for the door.

He beats her to the door. "How long did you sit out there and wait for me?" She shrugs without responding. "An hour two hours, for what reason just to ask me if I knew who killed your boss?" She stares at him wide-eyed and silent. "No, Miss Langston. I have no idea who did this. Not yet, but trust me. I will."

Quickly jotting a few notes in his ever-present notepad, Greg points at the chair the woman had just vacated. "I have a few more questions for you. Please sit back down."

She sighs, rubs at the scar and again shakes her head "there's nothing more that I can tell you."

Placing the pen on the table, taking his seat, Greg leans back in the straight-backed chair, interlacing his fingers behind his neck and stares up at her. "I know Armstrong wasn't born and raised in Cleveland. Where was he from?"

She stares back. "I honestly can't say."

He stands and leans across the table toward her, resting his hands on the table. "In all the years you worked for him, you never heard him say where he was from? Not even going back home on a vacation or for a death in the family, nothing like that?"

She stares at him with a blank look on her face. "Lieutenant, I was his office manager not his personal confidante."

Greg moves around the table towering over her. "You said you worked for him for ten years, but you can't tell me where he came from?"

She tilts her head to look up at him. "Are you attempting to intimidate me, Lieutenant? I assure you, it's not working. I can't tell you what I don't know."

He searches her face for some kind of answer, not finding one he asks her. "Are you from around here?"

She slips her purse strap over her shoulder stepping away from the table. "I am not."

Greg moved with her, blocking her

way. "Where are you from?"

Standing defiant in front of him, speaking in a soft voice, "Where I am from has nothing to do with Dr. Armstrong's death. If there's nothing else, may I go?"

Greg drew a deep breath, steps aside with a shrug. "Don't make any plans to leave town in the near future."

She moves around him, heading for the door. "Am I a suspect?"

He turns to watch her leave, but didn't try to stop her. "Anyone who knew the Armstrongs are suspects, including you."

Hand on the doorknob she stops in mid-motion, whirling angrily to face him. "I didn't have to come here tonight, but I did," she said through clenched teeth. "I didn't kill Doctor Armstrong and his wife and I don't know who did. You are a rude, presumptuous man, and I am leaving." She swung the door open and storms out of the room.

Greg follows her out of the building into the cool night air a thunder rumbled and a streak of lightening crackled overhead. "Miss Langston, I'm sorry if I offended you. But, this is not a simple traffic violation we're dealing with. It's a double homicide and the murderer is still out there. Who's to say you're not next on his list?"

A gust of wind from the impending storm whips around them and Greg smells rain in the air. Oblivious of the storm as she turns on him in anger and frustration, "then do your job, Lieutenant. Catch him."

The challenge she flung at him was like a slap and his head jerked in response. "Or maybe this is just too much for a small town police department to handle."

Regaining his composure, Greg hurries to catch up with her as she strode toward a dark blue Volkswagen Beetle parked at the curb. "You took the time to come in and talk to me. Why are you in such a hurry to leave now? I have more questions that only you can answer. Please, let's go back inside," he pleads.

The wind whips at her ponytail when she turns to face him. "Why should I? You don't believe what I've already told you. I have nothing further to say to you so unless you plan to arrest me on some trumped up charges, I'm leaving," she said grabbing her car keys from her purse, and flinging open the door of the little car.

The first cold raindrops beat down on his head as he held the door for her to enter the vehicle. "Thank you for coming in, Miss. Langston. I _will_ want to talk to you again in a day or two. Will you give me your address and phone number so I can reach you?"

She jerks the door from his grasp, slamming it on her response. "I'm in the phone book. Look it up." She glares at him through the window. "You can read, can't you?

She turns the key, put the car in gear and pulls away, Greg steps back to avoid having his toes run over. Standing in the downpour he watches as she turns the corner and out of sight.

"Beatrice Langston," he yells as lightening crackled and popped overhead, "I don't believe you. Your boss and his wife were murdered and you act like you don't give a fat rat's ass about it."

"Garrison," someone shouts from the open door of the police station, and he turns to see who it was. "In case you hadn't noticed," the uniformed officer yells to be heard over the thunder, "It's raining. Get in here, man."

Greg turns once more to peer in the direction Beatrice had gone then lopes for the cover of the building. "I don't believe you at all," he said once more as he ran through the door pulling it shut with a resounding slam.

Chapter Four

A new life in a tiny apartment in Cleveland, Georgia was the last place on earth Katherine—Kate to family and friends, O'Connor wanted to be at this particular moment in time. But, for now, she'd pretend contentment, regardless of whether she truly felt it or not because she was determined to prove her father, William O'Connor, Chief of Police of Clarke County in Athens, wrong. No matter what he said or felt, she <u>was</u> just as good at police work as he was— maybe better.

For years, he'd pestered her to attend the University of Georgia—constantly drilling it into her head that his alumnus was good enough for her brothers; therefore, it was certainly good enough for her. Reacting in the same way she'd always reacted to his nagging and bullying, Kate rebelled. She had no aspirations for college nor did she want to follow her mother's suggestion of finding a good man and starting a family like her sister Margie. In fact, Kate wanted to be married to some man who thought he knew more about her desires than she did even less than she wanted college. And having a bunch of snotty-nosed kids around all day was not her idea of a good life. Not now, probably not ever.

Mom seemed to find some sort of perverse pleasure in telling her she'd always been a problem child. "If you don't watch out," she'd say with a long-suffering sigh, "You'll come to no good."

Laughing good naturedly, Kate would give her a little hug before offering the same response every time the subject of the horrible end she was rushing toward came up. "Just because I'm not living my life according to Geneva O'Connor's rules doesn't mean I'm doomed. It's very possible that I can have a good life, Mom."

After much soul-searching, Kate submitted an application to the Clarke County Police Department and won a much-coveted seat in the academy. Although thrilled at the acceptance, she couldn't help but feel a twinge of resentment and anger at the nagging thought that her father's position within the department may have gotten her in, but she went anyway. She soared through the academy at the top of her class—pushing herself to be the best, to prove to herself and everyone else that she was worthy regardless of who her father was. And then finally graduation and that first assignment as a uniformed office— what a thrill. Four years later, she still loved her job and was conscientious, courteous, and thorough throughout every shift. Off duty; however, was a whole different story.

Kate adored parties and generally ran with a rough crowd that didn't care what she did to make her money. All they cared about was having a good time and as long as she played by their rules, she was accepted. Part of her worried about the drugs that were freely circulated and sold amongst this wild crowd—she was a police officer, she knew better. Deciding to turn a blind eye to the illegal activities, she told herself it was okay because <u>she</u> wasn't doing anything wrong. They were parties and she had no real control over what anyone else did, did she?

One night, feeling good after a few drinks and lots of crazy dancing, a strange man who introduced himself as Mr. Westmoreland approached her. Finding the formal introduction a bit out of place at such a gathering, she stepped back from his outstretched hand to study him carefully. He was slim, about five feet five inches tall, sandy blonde hair receding rapidly from a narrow forehead. Pale blue eyes stared back at her from a face that could only be described as peaches and cream—a complexion many women yearned for and probably envied on this odd man. Smiling to reveal too-white teeth that were obviously bleached, he acted as if they'd met before— as if he already knew her.

"How's the police business treating you, Miss O'Connor?"

"How do you know I'm a police officer? I'm sure we've never met before."

"We know many things about you. For instance, we know you've worked with the Clarke County Police Department for four years. You've completed several college courses because you want to become a detective. We also know that your daddy is the Chief of Police for this county." He shrugged. "Pretty common knowledge, don't you think? But now we think you're ready to hop out from under your daddy's wings and fly under your own power."

Kate smirked down at him. "So tell me something. Who is this 'we' you're talking about?"

Mr. Westmoreland raised an arm and pointed toward several of the guests scattered across the smoke-filled room who were free-basing crack, smoking marijuana, or cutting cocaine with small razor blades. "Why all of your lovely, law-abiding friends and me. That's who we are."

The smile he bestowed upon her didn't quite reach his eyes and Kate felt a slight tingle of apprehension in the pit of her stomach, but she tamped it down and stepped closer to the obnoxious little toad.

"What's your point? I don't do drugs."

The smile disappeared as quickly as it had come. "Miss. O'Connor, haven't you been present when these people make drug pick-ups and deliveries? Haven't you watched as they counted the money from drug sales?" Not waiting for the obvious response, he continued. "In fact, you have helped count money. Yet, you seem to feel comfortable claiming to have no connection to the 'we'."

"Listen, you little shrimp. Who do you think you're talking to? I could arrest you and everyone in this room right now if I wanted to."

He moved in closer, pale eyes glaring

up into hers, thin lips pressed even thinner in his anger. "True enough, I suppose. But keep in mind that you would probably be occupying a cell next to us—perhaps even <u>with</u> some of us."

"I'm clean. And you can't prove I've ever been anywhere around these people when they were dealing or using." She smirked down at him.

"Really? Start making arrests and find out. Not only do we have photographs that clearly show your presence and involvement, we also have video—you really are quite photogenic, my dear. You're up to your pretty little ear lobes in this. Like it or not."

The tingle of fear was back, spreading its talons through her stomach and up into her suddenly aching throat as she looked around the room at the people she thought were her friends, and then back to the man watching her with interest—looking at her as if she was a strange bug under a microscope.

"Why are you telling me this?"

"Now that's more like it." Stunned, Kate didn't protest when he grasped her firmly by the elbow, led her through the mass of sweaty, dancing bodies and out of the house to the far end of the long, vacant front porch.

"We have a situation in Cleveland, Georgia that we need you to take care of."

"What kind of situation?" she asked.

"First things first. The Cleveland Police are in the process of hiring a detective and we want you to apply for the position. With your four years on the force here and the college courses you've completed, we think you'll be accepted immediately. The fact that you're a woman won't hurt anything—equal opportunity and all that." He smiled playfully at her as he leaned against the porch railing and crossed his arms.

"How do you know Cleveland wants to hire another detective?"

"You are trying my patience, Miss O'Connor. How or what I know is not your concern."

"I don't want to move to Cleveland, Georgia. I'm not going to," Kate snapped.

Jumping forward faster than Kate thought possible; Westmoreland grabbed her, spinning her around, pushing her face into the corner, jerking her arm up hard behind her back. "Perhaps I haven't made myself clear," he growled against her ear. Kate smelled his foul breath as the pain shot up her arm and her heart jumped wildly in her chest. "You will do what you're told— when you're told." Jerking her arm a little further upward, he continued. "Now, do you understand?"

The pain was excruciating—for a moment Kate actually thought she might pass out. And for the first time in her life, Kate was afraid—for her safety, for everything she'd worked so hard to obtain, for her very life. Determined not to cry out, to give him the satisfaction of knowing he had hurt her, she closed her eyes against the pain and nodded. "I hear you," she whispered. "But I don't understand."

Westmoreland released her and stepped back as she whirled on him, eyes flashing anger as she rubbed her arm. He offered another of those smiles that didn't reach his ice-cold eyes.

"You like your freedom, right?" The threat in his tone was clear and Kate nodded a silent response. "Sure you do. You will do what you're told or you won't do anything at all. No questions. And right now you are being told to submit an application for the opening in Cleveland. Is that understood?"

Trembling in fear and frustration at the mess she'd gotten herself into, Kate stared silently back at him. He took one of her cold hands between both of his and laughed aloud when she quickly jerked it away.

"Don't be afraid, Kate. We've got big plans for you." Then he turned and walked

back inside the house, leaving her alone in
the darkness.

Chapter Five

As predicted, Kate reluctantly accepted
the position in Cleveland, which made her
Cleveland's second plain-clothes detective
as well as the first woman the department
ever hired. There'd been no word from
Westmoreland since their initial meeting at
the party, but he was out there—waiting,
watching. Then in late May, she received a
bulky envelope in the mail—no return
address, no indication of where it had come
from, but she knew. When she ripped it
open, a bundled stack of crisp twenty-dollar
bills tumbled out along with a typewritten
note stating she'd be receiving a package
shortly.

Thoughts tumbling over one another in
a rush, she tried to relax, to watch television
but even that mindless activity was
impossible. She simply could not
concentrate on anything. What could he
possibly be sending? After a hot bath, she
slipped into bed where she tossed and turned
until the sheets were a wrinkled mass
beneath her. Get up, she told herself, do
something, but she didn't. And finally,
sometime in the wee hours of the morning,
she drifted off to sleep, only to be awakened
a short time later by a persistent bang, bang,
bang. Sitting up with a jerk, heart pounding
madly in her chest, it took a moment for her
to realize someone was knocking on the
front door.

Stumbling down the short hallway and
crossing the living room, she flung open the
door to find a deliveryman standing there
with what she assumed to be the dreaded
Westmoreland package. Duly signed for, the
heavy box now sat on the kitchen table as
she paced around the room, looking at it one
minute, avoiding it the next, until at last she
decided to make a pot of coffee and shower
before doing anything else.

When she could put it off no longer, she
poured a cup of coffee, and breathed in the
heady aroma before seating herself at the

table in front of the package. With a sigh, she ripped it open, revealing a smaller box and a note instructing her to open it—expect a call soon was scribbled across the bottom of the page almost as an afterthought, which she knew was deliberate. The man left nothing to chance. Everything he did was very deliberate and carefully thought out.

Inside the smaller box was a gun with a silencer, a 9mm Luger, she noted automatically, a box of 123-grain cartridges and an empty clip. One by one, she lined the items up on the tabletop, opened the box of shells, then immediately closed it again and packed everything back in the box, crossing the room in quick strides to hide the offensive thing in the back of the closet under a jumble of old clothes and shoes. Satisfied that it wouldn't easily be discovered, she returned to the table, sipped at her now cold coffee with a grimace, dumped it into the sink, refilled the cup, and sat down at the table again to wait for Westmoreland's call—it was a short wait.

"Hello?"

"You get settled in your apartment okay?" It was him.

Enough small talk, she thought with annoyance. "Yes."

"Good. Let's get down to business, shall we. As I told you before, we have a problem down there that we want you to take care."

"What kind of problem?"

"Pay close attention because I only plan to tell you this once. Twenty years ago, one of my dealers—Philip Sharply, disappeared with twenty million dollars of my money. I'm a patient man so I simply waited. I knew he'd surface sooner or later or one of his associates would reveal. It finally happened.

"Mr. Sharply is living in Cleveland under the assumed name of Joseph Armstrong. Your assignment is to take him and his family out."

Gasping in disbelief, Kate shook her head even though the man on the other end of the phone couldn't see her. "No. No way. I'm not killing anyone for you or anyone else. Do you hear me?"

There was an odd, rasping noise from Westmoreland, which took Kate a minute to identify as a chuckle. "No need to shout, Kate. I'm not deaf. "

"I do have to shout. I'm not one of your hit men. I'm a police officer, for crying out loud!"

There was a slight pause on the other end. "Are you really so naïve as to think you're the only cop on our payroll?"

"I am not on your stinking payroll."

"What did you do with the money?"

She looked across the table at the crumbled envelope, the stack of new bills lying beside it where she'd left them and shook her head emphatically from side to side. "I don't want it."

"And yet you have it. Go out and have a good time with it or donate it to your favorite charity. You do have a favorite charity, don't you?" He didn't wait for her response. "I don't care what you do with it. The point is, you've got it. Therefore, you are on our stinking payroll."

Kate began to cry, the hot tears falling unchecked down her face to land with audible little plops against the tabletop. "I'm not a killer," she whispered.

"Are you crying, Kate? I thought you were tougher than that." Covering the mouthpiece, she sniffed loudly and swiped angrily at the tears on her cheeks, but offered no response.

"Under control again? Good. Now listen to me. You will be whatever we need you to be. If you won't, we have no use for you— dead or alive.

"I just wonder what Daddy would say if someone mailed him some pictures and an interesting video of his little party girl?"

An involuntary shiver ran along Kate's spine at the thought. "Is that a threat?"

Westmoreland laughed. "I don't make

threats, Kate. Just promises. Relax—no one will suspect you—you're a cop, remember."

"I'll know."

"Oh, come on, Kate. Did you think you could run with us and not get your hands dirty? I'm done talking. I expect the job to be finished before next weekend is over. And Kate only your life depends upon it."

"Hello? Hello? Don't you hang up on me, you bastard!" she shouted. The only response was the incessant buzz of the dial tone, followed after several moments by the sound of silence—he'd hung up.

Chapter Six

Tired to the point of exhaustion, she held the newborn close and ran her fingers through the baby's soft, brown curls. Smiling through a yawn, she whispers, "my precious little girl."

An elderly nurse, arms outstretched, appeared at the side of the bed almost as if by magic—first she was not there and then she was. "You'll see her later. She needs tending to right now," she said firmly as she removed the baby from the cradle of its mother's arms.

She wanted to protest to have just another moment with her daughter, but the sedative was beginning to take affect and she watched in silence until the nurse was out of sight. Pulling the blanket up under her chin to ward off a chill, she closed her eyes with a sigh. As she drifted toward a much-deserved sleep, she felt a presence at the side of the bed and opened her eyes once more.

A different nurse this time—dark-haired, a bit younger, a bit thinner, stared down at her. "You have company."

Fighting another yawn, she blinked several times in an attempt to focus on the woman's face. "Who is it?"

"Your parents."

"My parents?" That is impossible, she thought. Fighting to stay awake, to utter the words aloud, she shook her head from side to side. "Impossible," she muttered as the sedative kicked into high gear and she tumbled downward into a black, dreamless slumber.

Disoriented and alone, she awoke to a blinding flash of lightning and a boom-boom of thunder that shook the windows and momentarily dimmed the overhead lights. With shaking hands, she groped for the call button on the bedside table, and then pressed impatiently at the buttons with a long-nailed finger in an attempt to bring someone, anyone, into the room

A gray-haired nurse clad in a white uniform starched so stiffly that it crackled audibly with each step rushed into the room. Wresting the call button from the patient's hand, she offered an automatic smile that did not quite reach her dark eyes. "How can I help you?"

Still weak and tired, she struggled to sit upright in the bed. "I want to see my baby."

"Now, darlin', don't you fret about a thing. You're going to be alright," the nurse responded as she slowly injected a clear fluid into the intravenous line feeding into the back of the young woman's hand. Finishing, she deftly recapped the needle, dropped the syringe into a pocket of her uniform, and then placed two fingers against the cold skin of the patient's wrist to monitor her pulse. Once she had drifted back to sleep, the nurse turned and left the room, pulling the door shut behind her.

The next time she awoke, warm morning sunlight shone through the windows. Glancing down, she noticed a band-aid on the back of her left hand and wondered for a brief moment how it had gotten there. Still a bit groggy, she flipped back the covers and scooted to the foot of the bed. Heart doing a crazy thumpa-thumpa as her feet touched the cold floor, she stood still long enough to get her balance and glance around the unfamiliar room. How did I get here, she wondered as she brushed her long hair away from her face. Slipping into the hospital robe she found draped across the foot of the bed, she stumbled awkwardly into the hallway.

A hospital, she thought as she watched a maintenance man buffing the tile. The heavy buffer hummed quietly as he guided it from left to right and then back again, taking short steps, making sure not to miss a spot as he wove his expert way between patients slowly strolling the hall. To the left was a nurse's station. Clinging to the handrail extending the length of the hall, she shuffled in that direction, stopping several times in an attempt to clear her spinning head.

Head nurse, Agnes Fitzgerald, swung around in surprise as a sleepy voice behind her claimed, "I want to see my baby."

Staring in surprise at the sight of the patient from room 208 leaning against the wall, Agnes pushed her chair away from the desk and hurried to the young woman's side. "What are you doing out of bed? Let me help you back to you room." Grasping the young woman's slim arm firmly, she attempted to guide her back in the direction from which she had come.

"No. I want to see her now!"

Agnes was astonished at the young woman's strength. Even sedated, she was still strong enough to pull away. "Miss Armstrong. Brenda, please," Agnes pleaded as she placed her arm around her patient's small waist. Agnes looked into the woman's troubled eyes, took note of the heart-shaped face that was so pale it seemed as if Dracula might have used her for a late night snack— leaving little blood behind to sustain the body.

"I just want to see her," she pleaded tearfully as her tangled, unwashed hair tumbled over her eyes and she laid her weary head against the nurse's shoulder.

Agnes patted her back, and then began to lead her down the hall. "It's going to be alright. Let's just go down this way, shall we?"

Stopping several times to allow the patient to rest, Agnes wished for a wheelchair, but there was not one nearby. All of the other nurses and assistants were busy with their own patients so she continued the long, slow trek—half-carrying, half-supporting the by now exhausted patient. Attempting to hold her head up to see where she was going, the young woman breathed in short, sharp gasps—it seemed as if the sedative still had her in its grip. Her Jell-O legs felt as if they would not support her one more step. Surely she was about to collapse right here on the spot where her liquefied remains could quickly and efficiently be sucked up by a wet-dry vacuum.

"What's your name?" the young woman questioned as she gulped to pull enough air into her lungs.

"Mrs. Fitzgerald," Agnes, out of breath herself, huffed in response.

"Well, Mrs. Fitzgerald. I think I'm going to throw up."

Agnes felt her patient's stomach tighten as the first wave of nausea swept over her. Great, Agnes thought. If anything does come up, it will go right down the front of my fresh-from-the-cleaners uniform.

"Shit!" she whispered, breathing just as hard as the heaving young woman leaning against her. "Hold on, honey. We are almost there. Just a few more steps."

Stopping in front of an office, Agnes released her hold on the patient long enough to pound emphatically on the door. A muffled voice from inside answered and she turned the knob, pushing the door open with her foot. Grabbing for the young woman, who had began a slow slide toward the floor, she dragged her into the room and deposited her rather roughly into a Queen Anne's chair in front of the desk. Straightening her rumpled uniform, Agnes took several deep breaths before speaking.

"Sorry for the intrusion, but . . . ," shrugging, she nodded in the direction of the patient as if to say, "See for yourself."

"Brenda Armstrong, this is Dr. Hargrove."

Removing his wire-rimmed glasses, the doctor smiled at the young woman. "Ah, Miss Armstrong. Awake at last. How are you?"

Leaning against the back of the chair, Brenda swiped impatiently at her straggling hair. Her tongue felt heavy and useless in her mouth as she answered. "I would be fine if I could see my daughter."

Glancing up at the nurse, whose only response was a shrug, Dr. Hargrove frowned as he turned back to the patient. Before he could offer a response, she struggled to her feet and wobbled toward the desk. As her knees buckled, she grabbed for the edge of the desk to maintain her balance.

"I want to see her, now!"

Dr. Hargrove hurried around the desk to lead her back to the chair where she perched on the edge of the cushion. "Please, Miss Armstrong, we're here to help you."

Collapsing back into the chair, the frustrated young woman began to sob. "I just want my baby."

Kneeling next to her, the doctor patted her hand consolingly. "Do you remember anything that's happened to you?"

With a sigh, Brenda rested her head against the back of the overstuffed chair and closed her eyes in an attempt to make the spinning room come to a stop. "Yes. I am in the Northeast Georgia Medical Center. I had a baby. A little girl. And she's beautiful." Dr. Hargrove looked up at Mrs. Fitzgerald, who shook her head again in genuine confusion. Standing, he kept hold of the woman's hand. "Help me get her to the couch."

Drawing a deep, cleansing breath, Agnes walked briskly to the side of the chair where she placed her arm firmly under the confused woman's arm and around her back. With Dr. Hargrove positioned the same way on her other side, they lifted her to her feet and led her across the room.

"I feel so sorry for her. She has so much pain to face," Mrs. Fitzgerald stated as if Brenda could no longer hear them. Placing one of the small end cushions under the woman's head, she covered her with the light blanket, which had been draped over the back of the couch.

Frowning at the indiscretion, Dr.

Hargrove nodded. "I know. And we will help her to face that pain, starting right now." Settling onto the other end of the couch, Dr. Hargrove placed his feet solidly on the floor to emphasize his words.

Exhausted and confused, Brenda lay limply against the pillow—she wanted them to stop talking, longed to go to sleep. When she closes her eyes, terrifying images dance behind her eyelids. Panic engulfed her and her eyes flew open. She wanted to run, to find a safe place to hide, but she did not even have the strength to lift herself from the couch. Instead, frozen in fear, she lay still as death and listened to the voices around her.

Using a remote control, the doctor pressed the record button to start his video recorder. "Brenda, can you hear me okay?" he asked soothingly.

Eyes wide, Brenda stared upward without really seeing anything. Her stomach rumbled and churned as if there was an active volcano deep inside of her—it felt as if it would erupt at any moment, but she managed to keep it under control as she responded with a curt, "Yes."

"Can you tell me what you remember?"

Closing her eyes, she whispered so softly that he had to lean forward to catch her words. "My baby." Then, with an effort, she re-opened her eyes.

"What do you remember about your baby?" Dr. Hargrove asked, glancing up momentarily as Nurse Fitzgerald left the office and closed the door softly.

Brenda began to gasp for air, her breath coming in short, sharp gasps. "She was in my arms," she sobbed as she twisted a corner of the blanket between her hands. "In my arms."

Fearing that she was on the verge of collapse, he spoke firmly. "Brenda. Listen to me. I want you to calm down. Slow, deep breaths. No one is going to hurt you here. You are safe here. Do you understand?"

Her breathing rate increased as she twisted the blanket harder and faster. Her features contorted as she stared ceiling-ward with horror-filled eyes. "No. Not safe—not safe. They are going to kill my baby. We are not safe." At this point, she was sobbing so hard that he could barely understand the words that tumbled over one another in their rush to be spoken.

"Who are they, Brenda? Can you tell me?"

Tears coursed unchecked down her pale cheeks. "No. I want my baby. She is safe with me. I want my baby. They are going to kill her. I want her with me," she repeated over and over again.

"Brenda, why do you think you <u>have</u> a baby?"

The shock of his words brought her back to reality for a moment and she stared at him as if he were the one who needed help. "Because I was holding her. A nurse came into the room and took her away. Where is she? I want my baby!"

Dr. Hargrove moved closer to disentangle the blanket from between her cold fingers, and then held her hands tightly between both of his. She struggled against his grasp for a moment before giving in— willing herself to relax a bit.

"It's okay. See? I am not going to hurt you. I want to help you. Can you stop crying for me so I can do my job?"

His touch, the tone of his voice did make her feel safer—not completely safe, but enough so that she drew a deep breath before looking deep into his eyes. "I'll never see her again!" she whispered. "They'll kill her!"

"Who will, Brenda?" He sensed her control slipping away again.

Shaking her head weakly, she began to sob again. "I . . . I don't know. Please help me. Please. They're going to kill her."

Not speaking for long moments, he rubbed her hands between his as he waited for the sobs to subside. He sensed her inner struggle, her desire to regain control and took it as a good sign. "Brenda, try to clear your mind. Do not think about anything but the sound of my voice. Okay?"

"Yes."

Handing her a box of tissues from a nearby table, he nodded before continuing. "I need you to remember something. Will you help me?"

Raising a shaky hand to her face, she swiped at the tears and sniffed loudly. Maybe it was the cleansing flood of tears or the overwhelming sense of doom she felt or the combination of the two, but something was working to clear the after affects of the sedative from her system. She felt more awake, more alert; than she had since the moment the nurse took her tiny daughter from her arms and walked out of the room with her.

"I'll try if you think it will help.

"I need you to think back to the time before you had a baby. What do you remember?"

Jerking her hands from his, she clenched her fists, staring at him defiantly. "I don't understand. All I remember is holding my baby."

He wanted to get her past this moment without sending her into a tailspin, which would cause her to refuse to speak with him at all. "What about your parents? Do you remember them?"

Turning her face away from him, she focused her gaze on the ceiling and shook her head. "They're not here," she whispered.

"Where are they?"

"Dead. They're both dead."

"How did they die, Brenda?" He leaned toward her, ready to offer whatever comfort he could should she have a sudden flash of insight—some small memory of what might have happened.

"I . . . I'm not sure. Was it an accident?"

"Was it? What kind of accident do you

think it might have been?"

Closing her eyes tightly again, she shook her head from side to side and answered through clenched teeth. "A car accident,"

"Okay. Relax now. You are still safe. You're here in my office with me." He paused to let his words sink in. "Were you with them?"

She pressed her thin lips together, tight, tighter, and tighter still until all the color drained from them and they were as pale as the surrounding flesh. Not speaking, she simply shook her head from side to side.

This is not a hallucination, he thought as he watched a range of emotions from fear, to anger, to dismay, and then back to fear dance rapidly across her face. She is remembering something. "How old were you when the accident happened?"

Grabbing the blanked, she pulled it up tightly under her chin just as a small child might who was seeking comfort from a bad dream. "I don't know."

So fragile, he thought. So very, very fragile, but he pressed on... "Do you remember attending the funeral?"

Quite unexpectedly, she started kicking her feet and swinging her arms wildly as if trying to ward off an unseen attacker. The frenzy stopped as quickly as it had started and she jerked the blanket up over her head as she cowered against the back of the couch, screaming. "No! No! No! Noooo! I don't want to talk about this! Just give me my baby. Give me my baby!"

Pressing the remote control again to stop the recording, he rose to his feet. "Stop, Brenda. We won't talk any more right now. I'll have you taken back to your room. A nurse will give you something to help you rest."

As he turned toward his desk, he thought he heard her mumble something against the back of the couch. "Brenda? Did you say something?"

Lowering the blanket, she turned her tear-stained, swollen face toward him. "I don't have a baby, do I?"

Wishing he could tell the heart-broken, troubled young woman she did indeed have a child, that she was merely experiencing a bad dream from which she would awaken shortly and be happy, he shook his head. Sometimes this job was so hard, so damned hard. "No", he responded softly. "I'm sorry. There is no baby."

"But it was so real. I held her in my arms—smelled her baby sweetness, ran my fingers through those soft curls. What is happening to me? Am I losing my mind?"

Helping her to an upright position, he reseated himself on the couch and smiled reassuringly. "No, you're not losing your mind. Something happened to you and I'm trying to help you remember what it was so that you can get past it."

For the first time, he really looked at her eyes and found himself fascinated by the unusual color—pale brown with tiny flecks of gold. She stared back for a moment before blinking and looking around the room in confusion.

"Where am I? I mean, what hospital am I in?"

What was this? She knew where she was—had told him that on her own when she first came into the room. Unsure of her reasoning, he answered anyway. "You're at the Gainesville Sanitarium in Georgia. My name is Dr. Henry Hargrove. I'm a psychiatrist. I want to help you. Miss Armstrong, Brenda, I will not pressure you to remember anything you're not ready for." Perhaps she was simply seeking reassurance and that's what he offered.

Staring into his eyes, she nodded in agreement. "Okay, but why are you calling me Miss Armstrong? Brenda? Do you think I'm her?"

Now this was a new twist. He tilted his head to one side and looked at her with renewed interest. "Are you saying you're not Brenda Armstrong?"

"No, of course I'm not. I'm Brenda's half sister, Bethany Akin."

Chapter Seven

This case was bad one, perhaps the worst the tiny town had ever seen, with very few clues to indicate who might have committed such a horrific crime or why. It was imperative that Greg speak with the young woman who may well have seen or heard something that could help. Patience were Greg's strong point, he paced back and forth in the hallway outside of the doctor's office. <u>Hurry</u>, he thought, <u>hurry</u>. He'd wait all day if he had to, but no one could make him like it.

Just as he thought he'd scream in frustration, Dr. Hargrove opened the door and extended a hand in greeting. "Lieutenant Garrison. You wanted to see me?"

Greg clasped the doctor's hand firmly then pulled a battered notepad from the back pocket of his khakis and strode through the open door. "Yes sir."

A hand to his mouth covered a smile of amusement at the younger man's obvious impatience Dr. Hargrove reentered the office, closed the door and crossed the room to sit behind the paper-strewn desk. Motioned Greg to the nearest chair, then he propped his elbows on the desk and rested his chin atop his clasped hands.

"I want to thank you, Dr. Hargrove, for taking time out of your busy day to meet with me."

"You're quite welcome. I just hope I can help in some way."

In no hurry now that he was inside the office, Greg took a moment to size up the doctor—to get a feel for what type of man he was dealing with here. Somewhere in his mid-fifties, hair more salt than pepper, the doctor wore both jacket and tie, which Greg thought looked rather uncomfortable. Why didn't he remove the jacket, loosen the tie? Couldn't he relax in his own office? Even though the doctor was now seated, Greg guessed him to be about five foot nine or so, slender build—all in all, not a bad looking guy. Maybe a bit stuffy, but he seemed cooperative enough.

Greg quickly surveyed the room, taking note of the iron bars covering the windows––fairly standard for older institutions such as this one, but uncommon in newer facilities where the patients were usually so drugged they never gave a thought to escape—or anything else for that matter. Degrees from various universities and colleges hung in neat rows along one wall and pictures of the doctor with a woman Greg assumed was his wife, and two young girls, who clearly resembled their father, sat on the desk. There were also two separate photos of the girls—both were formal studio shots with the girls clad in identical graduation caps and gowns.

Hargrove's big oak desk, complete with a recessed control panel and built-in microphone, faced the door. A large, expensive-looking beige rug covered part of the oak-paneled floor. A buttery-soft leather couch ran the length of one wall, and three chairs, upholstered in matching mauve fabric were placed strategically about the room. Opposite the couch was an entertainment center, replete with rows and rows of books, a large television, and a videocassette recorder. There was also a recessed camera in the ceiling, turned off at this point, but ready to focus on the couch's occupant at the press of a button. Patient sessions must be recorded he thought to himself.

Finished with his visual inventory taking, Greg turned his attention back to the doctor, who had watched in bemusement as his guest "checked out" his surroundings. "Has she said anything about what happened?"

Leaning back in his chair, Dr. Hargrove shook his head. "No."

Greg removed a ballpoint pen from his shirt

pocket, tapped it against the note pad open on his leg. "I don't suppose I could speak with her?"

"She's still very confused. She believes her parents were killed in a car accident."

"Based on your extensive experience, do you think she's telling the truth? Or is she trying to scam you?"

Ignoring the question for the moment, Dr. Hargrove continued. "She also claims she is not Brenda Armstrong."

Greg stopped tapping the pen and stared at him in confusion. "Excuse my ignorance, Doc, but, huh? Why?"

Dr. Hargrove leaned forward again, placed his elbows on the desk. "I think she's telling the truth. She's not Brenda Armstrong."

"Then who is she?"

"Brenda's half sister, Bethany Akin."

Greg thoughtfully tapped his front teeth with the pen for a moment before responding. "Does she have any ideas about where Brenda might be?"

"I didn't ask her yet. I think Miss Akin wants to talk about what she saw in that house, but she's not ready."

Dr. Hargrove stood and walked around the desk and perched on the edge of it. "Lieutenant, I know it's imperative that you speak with Miss Akin, but I need a few more days with her."

Greg also stood and nodded, recapped the pen, put it back in his shirt pocket and crammed his little notebook in the back pocket of his khakis. "I've got plenty of other things to check out. And I doubt Miss Akin will be going anywhere any time soon."

"It sounds as if she's one of your suspects."

Greg shrugged. "Everyone who knew these people are suspects."

The men were silent for a moment, and then Greg extended his hand. "Thanks for your time. Let me know when I can talk to her."

"Certainly," Dr. Hargrove replied, shaking the proffered hand. Greg nodded once more, turned and let himself out of the office.

Chapter Eight

Greg found himself once again sitting in front of the house where the murders were committed, he gave himself a mental shake––it was time to stop concentrating on what he didn't know and pay attention to the here and now. Maybe, just maybe, there was something they'd missed in the initial investigation that would shed some light on the murders, but he'd never find anything if he didn't pay attention.

He knew the state police search had been thorough—they'd gone through the house room by room, canvassed the neighborhood and surroundings areas asking questions and searching for the murder weapons—all to no avail. But you never could tell. It was possible they'd overlooked something, a tiny detail that could help the investigation. There was no harm in looking again, and again, and then again if necessary.

By this time he was in the upper hallway, ready to enter the master bedroom. As he reached for the doorknob, the cell phone fastened to his belt rang, a startling noise in the otherwise too silent house.

"Garrison here."

"Where are you?" Chief Boswell barked into his ear.

"At the Armstrong house, what's up?"

"The search warrant for Armstrong's office is on your desk. When do you expect to be here?"

"Great! I'm on my way now." Forgetting about the search of the house for the time being, he retraced his steps, almost running down the stairs in his hurry to return to the station.

"Did you talk to Hargrove?" Boswell asked.

"Yeah," Greg answered as he ran from the house and practically leapt into his car.

"What happened?"

"I'll tell you about it when I get there."

* * *

He'd stopped at the front desk long enough to retrieve his messages, but simply tossed them unread onto a growing stack of paperwork when he reached his desk. Removing his jacket, he slung it across the back of his chair and reached for the warrant. Before he got a chance to skim over the contents, Chief Boswell was standing at his side.

"Well?"

"Well, what?" Greg responded as he pulled out the worn leather chair with a grimace and sat, squirming a bit as he tried to get comfortable despite the rips and cracks in the seat cushion. "What about a new chair, boss?"

Boswell ignored him. "What happened with the doctor?" Boswell asked, perching on the edge of the desk.

"Want to hear something really weird?" He didn't expect a response and didn't wait for one. "According to him, Brenda Armstrong is not Brenda Armstrong after all. She's her half sister, Bethany Akin, who thinks her parents were killed in a car accident."

"Okay—and what do you think?"

"I'm not sure. I guess it's possible but why didn't the neighbors know who she was? They called her Brenda—all of them did.

"The doc wants a few more days with her and then I can go back for a visit. Any word from Nesbit yet? Has he finished the autopsies?" He pushed the chair further away from the desk so he could cross his long legs and stretch his arms high over his head as he yawned hugely.

Shaking his head, Boswell stood and yawned himself. "I spoke with him earlier. Nothing for us yet."

"I have a bad feeling in my gut about all this." Greg said.

"Take an antacid."

Much as he tried to ignore her, Greg couldn't help noticing a woman seated a few desks away. Tall, slender, dark-haired and dark-eyed, she was dressed all in different shades of pink, she leaned forward, elbows on the desk, trying to hear every word being said by the two men. <u>Very pretty</u>, Greg thought<u>. And very nosy. Why does she think our conversation is any of her business?</u>

"Who <u>is</u> that?" Greg asked.

"You like her?" Boswell teased.

"She's cute enough, but what's she doing here?" Greg asked, turning his back to the woman and sitting up a little straighter in the chair.

"She's our newest employee."

Greg looked at Boswell, then at the woman, and then back at Boswell again. "Really? I didn't know we had an opening. What will she be doing?"

With a chuckle, Boswell got to his feet, motioning with his hand for the young woman to join them. "She's your new partner."

Greg was on his feet in an instant, head shaking in angry protest. "Huh uh. No way. I don't work with a partner."

An attempt to hold in his laughter failed and Boswell guffawed loudly. "You do now."

Greg ignored the hand she held out toward him as she approached, turning instead to the chief, who was busy wiping tears of glee from his eyes. "I'm glad you're getting a kick out of this", Greg said with disgust. "But it's not happening—no way. I don't have time to train a rookie."

Laughter gone as quickly as it had appeared, Boswell raised an eyebrow as if to say, oh really, before responding to the detective's protests. "When the Commissioner calls and tells me to hire another detective, I don't argue, fuss, or tell him I don't need one. I do as I'm told.

"So I reviewed all of the applications— about two dozen or so, and there was one that really stood out. Hers. I offered her the job and she accepted."

"This is my case and I'll solve it. I don't need a partner!" Greg stormed back.

Boswell stepped forward so he and the angry detective were standing toe to toe though he still had to look up into the other man's face. "Listen to me, Garrison. I'm your boss so if I say you have a partner, then you have a partner.

"Now let me introduce you two. This is Katherine O'Connor; call her Kate for short. Kate, this is Greg 'the Moose' Garrison." Boswell effectively ended the conversation by turning on his heel and returning to his office where he promptly slammed the door against any intrusions.

"You could've asked me first. I hate being called Moose," Greg shouted.

Kate rapped her knuckles against his desk to get his attention. "I don't need you to hold my hand. My personal file is on your desk." She looked at the files and papers scattered across the desktop with disgust. "Somewhere in all that mess," she added. Her voice was husky as if she smoked too many cigarettes and drank too much cheap whiskey. Very interesting and very sexy, Greg thought then forgot his annoyance at Boswell and turned to her with a little more interest.

Maybe I should straighten up this desk, he thought as he scanned the mess looking for anything resembling a personal file. Not finding it, he grabbed a stack of phone messages and began skimming through them. "Yeah, sure. Hi, how are 'ya?"

Kate smiled and he felt his heart do a little two-step in his chest. It was the kind of smile that would make a man do anything for her—make him offer anything just to keep it on her face. And she'd shared it with him. Him, Greg Garrison, and for a long moment he simply stared at her, forgetting the messages clasped in his hands, the warrant on his desk, and everything else but the joy of that smile.

"So, do I call you Greg or Moose?"

The smile was gone and he wanted to beg her to please give him another but had enough sense left in his addled brain to know she'd think he was crazy if he did. Choosing, instead to toss the unread messages on top of a stack of papers in the in basket on the corner of the desk, he shrugged. "My name is Greg so that's what you call me." He could feel the eyes of the other officers in the room watching him— knew they were snickering and jabbing each other in the ribs with sharp elbows without turning to look at them.

"So how did you get the name Moose?" she asked, taking a seat in the chair at the end of his desk and crossing her long, slim legs.

With an exaggerated sigh of disgust, Greg shook his head as someone behind him snickered. "Oh, jeez! I'll tell you if you promise not to mention it again. I hate that stupid nickname."

"Sure."

"When I was in high school, I played football. No defensive line could hold me back. No matter how big those guys were I'd run right through them, which earned me the nickname Greg 'the Moose.' You know, because I ran over everyone like a charging moose. Now, can we get down to more serious business?"

"He still charges into everything," someone called out as the other men laughed.

A uniformed officer stepped over to the desk, nodding in Kate's direction. "Don Loy," he offered by way of an introduction before turning to Greg. "But when you started working here part time, you went from a moose to a gopher. Didn't you Greg?"

The men all laughed loudly as Kate offered a tiny version of her earlier smile— not half the wattage behind this one as the first, Greg noted as he watched her face. It wasn't <u>that</u> funny, she thought. Men are so weird sometimes.

Greg glared at the pudgy officer. "Don't you have a ticket to write or something?" Not insulted in the least, Loy laughed and shuffled back towards the other officers, who clapped him on the back and gave him high-fives.

"So, tell me something about Katherine—Katc O'Connor." Greg said.

"Well, I'm from Athens, Georgia and I've worked with the Clarke County Police Department for the last four years. I've been taking some law enforcement classes at the University of Georgia—actually that's where I heard about the position here. I applied because I've always wanted to be a detective. And that, as they say, is that. Here I am."

"Very nice. Anything else you want to add to your resume?"

She met his gaze. "Yeah. My father is the Chief of Police in Athens. Before that, he was a detective and so was my grandfather before him. I know the ropes because I've been trained by the best of the best. So why don't we get to work?"

"Yes, sir…I mean ma'am," Greg said saluting her. "Congratulations on your accomplishments. I know we're going to make a good team. Okay?" He held out his hand, she placed her smaller one in it and they shook.

"Thank you. The search warrant for Armstrong's office is on your desk, remember?"

"Let's go," Greg said, locating the warrant amidst the clutter and snatching it up.

Greg offered to drive since he didn't know whether or not Kate had learned her way around the small town yet or not. As he led her to his car she let out a low whistle. "Nice ride," she said as she ran a hand over the leather seat. "What do have in it? A 302?"

"I'm impressed. You know police work

and cars, huh? My kind of woman," he teased. "Actually, yeah, that's what's under the hood. I wanted to restore it as close to the original as possible.

"Let's get this show on the road, Kate. Did you read the case file?"

"Yes, as far as it goes." They were silent as Greg drove slowly through town, then suddenly Kate pointed. "There's the street."

"I know where the street is."

"Just trying to help," she mumbled.

Greg parked, got out of the car and approached a tall lanky man standing at the curb. The guy's dark hair was slicked back from his forehead with enough oil to fry chicken in and he had one of the biggest noses Greg had ever seen. It was almost impossible not to stare at that nose as he asked, "Are you the owner?"

"Yeah. Are you the police?"

"That would be us. I'm Lieutenant Greg Garrison and this is . . . what are you anyway?" he asked, turning to Kate.

"I'm Sergeant Kate O'Connor," she responded as she extended a hand to the thin man. He ignored her as he concentrated on removing a key from a large ring attached to his belt by a silver chain.

"I don't get involved with my tenants," he explained as he finally managed to free the key. "The guy said he was a doctor. He paid his rent on time every month and that's all I cared about."

"Sure it is. Here's the search warrant. May I have the key?"

He dropped it into Greg's outstretched hand. "Here it is. If you lose it, I'm billing the county for the cost of having another one made." He snatched the warrant from Greg's other hand and stormed off.

"Have a good day," Greg yelled at his retreating back, and then mumbled "Creep" under his breath before entering the building followed closely by Kate.

They toured the almost empty office

space where the walls in the back room were lined with filing cabinets. Greg opened one to reveal a pile of dust and a lone spider busily weaving a web in hopes of catching an early dinner. Turning to a nearby desk, he pulled open a drawer to find empty space.

Kate watched in disbelief from the doorway. "What do you think?"

Greg shook his head as he opened and closed the rest of the desk drawers and pulled open several of the filing cabinets drawers as well. "Look at all of this dust. These cabinets have never been used."

"Yeah, that's pretty obvious. What do you think Armstrong really did here?"

"I'd be willing to bet my pension that he wasn't a doctor," he said as he brushed past Kate to return to the reception area. There was a single cabinet here and he opened a drawer to find several folders inside.

"Probably phony patients for a phony doctor," he mumbled, looking inside the first folder.

Removing a second folder, Kate flipped through the notes inside looking for a phone number. "Let's see. Patient's name is Beverly Arnold—husband's name is Leon. No phone number but information might have something."

Pulling a cell phone from her purse, she dialed information, when an operator answered she asked for a phone number and address of Leon Arnold. The operator told her there were three listings and Kate hastily scribbled all of them down in a tiny notepad she retrieved from a side pocket of the purse. "Thanks for your help."

"None of them match the address or phone number listed here but they could have moved and changed the number. It happens all of the time."

"Good thinking, rookie, "

Kate dialed the first number on her list. "May I speak with Beverly Arnold?" She gave Greg a thumbs-up to indicate she'd hit the jackpot on the first try.

Greg leaned against the desk beside Kate, arms crossed over his chest as he listened to her side of the conversation.

"Mrs. Arnold, my name is Sergeant Kate O'Connor. I'm a detective with the White County Police. We're investigating the murder of Dr. Joseph Armstrong and his wife. Did you know Dr. Armstrong?"

"No. I never heard of him until I read about the murders in the paper. My God, it's just horrible—why are you calling me?"

"Our investigation has turned up a file with your name on it—husband's name is Leon, right?"

"That's my husband's name. But, I never met that man. Neither had Leon."

"The address and phone number in the file are different from the listing I got from information. May I ask how long you've lived at your current location?"

"My goodness. We bought this land from old man Wilson forty years ago and built our first house a few yards from where the newer one is now. We raised five children here."

"Thank you, Mrs. Arnold. I appreciate your help."

"We're not in trouble, are we?"

"No, ma'am, just a routine call. Again, thanks for your time."

"I hope you find whatever it is you're looking for. Goodbye."

Taking the useless folder from her hand, Greg tossed it onto the floor. "Like I said, a phony doctor."

"Have you worked a lot of homicides?" Kate asked as she crossed the room to retrieve another folder.

"Nope, thank goodness." Pulling a crumpled map from the back pocket of his slacks, he spread it across the desk, using Kate's cell phone as a paperweight to hold it flat. "But, I'm not some dumb country bumpkin either. I attended Georgia State University to get my degree in criminology. And I've been with the county police for eight years."

"That's great. Ok—tell me what went through your mind when you got to the crime scene?"

Silent for a long moment, he stared down at the map without seeing a thing. Finally, he lifted his head to meet her penetrating gaze. "I'm not going to lie to you. This case scares the hell out of me. It's one thing to see the pictures and read the report, but it's quite another to see the murder scene up close and personal. We need to be very careful." He turned back to study the map again

"I agree with you, Greg," she answered softly.

"Thanks, Kate. You worked with Clarke County for four years so you know the routine. Don't let anything get past you. If someone passes you information, verify it. Don't take any shortcuts when you review evidence. If you need a search warrant, get it before you enter a place or remove any evidence—we don't want to lose anything on a technicality. If you're not sure of what needs to be done, ask me.

"When we catch the murderer, and we will catch him, I don't want the charges dismissed because we screwed up somewhere along the way."

"That's just standard operating procedure. You know, you may be right about Armstrong." Putting the folders aside, she crossed the room to study the lone certificate hanging in a cheap, plastic frame on the otherwise bare wall. "I wonder if this is phony too."

Joining her, Greg removed the frame from the wall to study the piece of paper more closely. "A certificate from the Medical College of Georgia, in Augusta does not a doctor make. I guess this, along with using the title of doctor made him feel more like the real thing. Just one more clue to check out, I guess. He tossed the framed certificate onto the stack of folders on the floor, planning to take everything back to the station when they returned.

"Do you think it could have been a mob hit, Greg?"

"Too messy. It would've been one shot to the head, not four shots to each victim. Besides, they wouldn't have left a witness.

"Even though there were eight shots fired, not one neighbor heard a thing, which means our killer probably used a silencer. No one heard a cry for help either. And they never saw anyone enter or exit the house until the girl, who says she's not Brenda Armstrong, came screaming out onto the lawn. I have a gut feeling she's involved somehow."

"Wasn't she injured?"

Greg shrugged. "I've cut myself worse shaving," Bending, he gathered the stack of evidence from the floor before continuing. "No cancelled checks, no bank statements, no nothing, right?"

With a final glance around the room, Kate nodded in agreement "right."

Greg pulled the cell phone from his belt and began punching in numbers. "Time to call the oh-so-cooperative Miss Langston." He listened as a recorded message informed him that the number he had dialed was no longer in service.

"What a surprise. Her phone's been disconnected."

"What now?"

"Let's go pay her a visit. I've got the address down in my car. Let's hope she hasn't had time to skip town.

"Damn it. I knew she was hiding something when I talked to her on Saturday night. Grab that map, will you? There's nothing else we need here." Pulling the door closed and locking it behind them, Greg followed Kate down the stairs and out of the building.

Chapter Nine

"Langston came to see you?" Kate asked, fastening her seat belt.

"Yeah. And it seemed pretty obvious that she was hiding something."

"Another question. Why wasn't the gun or the knife included on the inventory list?"

Greg didn't respond as he merged into the heavy traffic on Highway 129, heading north—hopefully to find Langston before she realized he was looking for her. Checking the rearview mirror, he changed lanes, sped up, and then favored Kate with a glance.

"We never found them . . . not in the house, the neighborhood . . . nowhere."

"Doesn't that put a great big hole in your theory that the girl is the murderer?"

He shook his head. "Not at all. There could have been an accomplice," Turning on the turn signal, he maneuvered into the right hand lane, exited the highway, and took a left onto Mountain Laurel Road, where supposedly Beatrice Langston lived.

"That's a mighty big stretch of the imagination," Kate continued. "It just sounds too convenient to place the blame on her."

He glanced over at her and then turned his attention back to the winding road. "The bloody footprints leading from the kitchen through the foyer and out the front door belonged to Bethany Akin—or whoever she is.

"The neighbors didn't go into the kitchen. They could see straight into the kitchen from the front foyer and stopped when they saw the bodies. The police wore shoe booties and laid a tarp on the floor so the crime scene wouldn't get contaminated."

"Here we are," he said, turning abruptly into a dirt and gravel driveway.

The storybook white wood frame house complete with a long porch across the front and a white picket fence, nestled in a grove of large oak trees.

The driveway was dotted with puddles from the recent rain, but the luxuriant green lawn was dry. The house was surrounded by an abundance of boxwood shrubs and a huge bed of blooming roses, their heady aroma scenting the air, occupied a big part of the yard. Tall cedars grew along the road while a huge white oak offered shade to the house and side yard.

"Not bad for an office manager," Greg noted as they mounted the stairs to the front door. "How much do you think she makes a year?" Kate shrugged as she attempted to peer through a front window and Greg rapped loudly on the door with his knuckles.

"If you're looking for the Langston woman, you're too late. She moved out yesterday."

Startled, they both turned to see a woman in her mid-seventies clad in a loose, faded sundress and an oversized straw hat leaning against a hoe as she watched them with some interest from across the picket fence.

Stepping from the porch, they approached her from across the lawn. "Did you know her very well?" Greg asked.

"Nah, she wasn't the neighborly type."

"How long did Miss Langston live here?" Kate asked raising a hand to her face to shade her eyes from the too bright morning sun.

"About nine or ten years I guess—pretty long time."

Greg flipped open his note pad and looked at her, pen poised. "You said she moved out yesterday?" The old woman nodded. He waited for more information but none was forthcoming. The stoop-shouldered woman simply leaned heavily on the hoe, peering up at him from under the brim of the wide hat.

"Did she use movers or did she do it herself?"

"Far as I could tell, she only took her clothes. No need for movers to do that."

Not wanting to offend the woman, but thinking she might be confused, Kate turned and spoke softly to Greg. "Maybe she didn't move."

Shifting her gaze from one to the other, the old woman snorted in disgust. "I may be old, Missy, but I'm not hard of hearing. She's gone.

"Her landlord came over last night to ask me if I might know of anyone who needed furniture or anything else for that matter. He said she called to let him know she was moving out and didn't want any of the things in the house—suggested he sell everything and keep the money or give it away because she wouldn't be in touch again."

"How long have you lived here?" Greg asked, taking notes.

Ignoring the question, the old woman pointed an arthritic finger at Greg, faded blue eyes sparkling in recognition, "I know you. Ain't you Mary and Alvin Garrison's boy?"

"Yes, ma'am," he answered and stopped writing to look at her more closely. Was this woman someone he should know?

Stepping closer, she reached across the fence to place a gloved hand upon his arm. "Well, son, you ought to know me. I'm Alberta Deerfield. My boy and your daddy went to school together. You know him too, William Deerfield. Of course, we call him Bill."

Removing her work gloves, she dropped them into a pocket of her dress and held out her hand, which Greg took carefully between both of his.

"Yes, ma'am I went to school with your grandson, Michael. It's been a long time since I saw you last."

"That's right." She waved her hand toward the house and surrounding property. "Mr. Deerfield bought this land some sixty odd years ago. We have over a hundred acres here."

She nodded toward the house that Miss Langston had so recently vacated. "We sold two acres to Mr. Clinton Brooks back in the early sixties and he's the one who built that house. His wife died of cancer, poor thing; that happened in '70 or '71."

"Clinton tried to live in the house after she passed, but there were too many ghosts of her hanging around, I guess. He couldn't deal with the memories.

"He moved to Gainesville and rented the house first to one family, and then another; until about ten years ago when Miss Langston moved in. That's about all I can tell you."

She leaned forward, using the hoe as a cane to keep her balance and peered closely at Greg's face. "Lord, you look like your daddy, got that thick auburn hair just like him. Got his height too—you got any kids yet?"

"No, ma'am I'm not married."

"A good-looking man like you what's the problem? You ain't getting any younger, you know. How old are you, anyway?"

Feeling the heat of embarrassment rising in his face, he replied, "I'm thirty."

"My word! If you had a kid right now, you'd be 'bout ready for your old age pension by the time it got to be twenty years old. You aren't one of those funny boys, are you? You know, the kind that don't like women?"

"No, I'm not one of those funny boys. I like women just fine." His face grew even warmer and he turned quickly to Kate as a way to change the direction the conversation was taking.

Frowning at the grin of amusement on her face, he pulled her forward by one arm so she stood directly in front of the older woman. "This is my partner Kate O'Connor. We're detectives with the White Sheriff's Police Department. We're investigating the murder of Joseph Armstrong and his wife.

"Miss Langston said she was his office

manager and we came out here to ask her a few questions. Looks like we missed her." The words came out in a rush and the women exchanged a puzzled look before returning their gazes to his face.

"You all will have to forgive me, but I need to sit down. Come on up to the porch for a minute." Without waiting to see if they'd obey her command, Mrs. Deerfield crossed the yard to clamber slowly up the steps. Removing her hat, she tossed it onto the porch before carefully settling herself into an old, wooden rocker.

"I heard about that on the news. I don't know what's happening in the world anymore." She changed topics almost in mid-sentence. "Miss Langston never got used to living in the country."

Kate had followed her up onto the porch where she leaned against the railing but Greg chose to remain on the stairs. "How's that?" he questioned.

"She never worked in her yard. If she needed anything done she hired someone to do it.

"Every Friday afternoon as regular as the sun went down, she would hop into whatever car she happened to be driving at the time and leave—always took the same little overnight case and always stayed gone until the following Monday afternoon. She did that for ten years without fail. Peculiar person." The old lady rested her head against the back of the chair and slowly began to rock.

Greg and Kate shared a small smile— here's a woman with a lot of time on her hands Kate's eyes seemed to say. He nodded in agreement and flipped silently through his notes for a minute, enjoying the lazy creak-croak, creak-croak of the chair as it moved back and forth.

"We really do need to get back to work. But, could you tell me how to get in touch with the owner of the house?"

She stopped rocking and leaned

forward. "Well, old man Brooks died a couple of years ago. His stepson, John Bolden, took over the house. He lives over near Blood Mountain. Nice fellow, you'll like him." She closed her eyes and resumed rocking.

"Thank you, Mrs. Deerfield, for all of your help," Greg said as he began walking across the yard back to his car. Kate quickly caught up with him and gave him a little wink, which made his heart skip a beat.

"You're welcome. Say hello to your folks for me."

"Are we getting a search warrant for the house?" Kate asked as they climbed into the car and Greg backed out onto the road.

His mind raced almost as fast as he was drove. "I suppose we should but as clean as she left the office, I doubt we'll find anything. She's not stupid enough to leave evidence lying around the house for us to find and use against her."

He took a curve too fast, running off the road on her side. Kate felt the car slide in the loose gravel and grabbed for the dashboard to steady herself seconds before Greg got the car back under control. "What fire are we going to?"

"Sorry about that." He slowed down a bit. "She has a three-day head start on us. She could be in Egypt by now."

They sat in comfortable silence for a few minutes, Kate watching the passing scenery and Greg darting glances at her lovely profile as he drove. "Another thing" he said at last. "This is an election year and if I know Thomas Clayton the way I think I do, he's already been on the phone to Chief Boswell wanting to know if we have anyone in custody.

"Cleveland is a small town but it still has its politics. Clayton will put pressure on Boswell, and he, in turn will put demands on me. I don't like pressure. Do you understand where I'm coming from?"

Nodding, she relaxed against the soft

leather of the seat. "Don't they understand it takes time to solve a crime like this?"

Greg shook his head. "They don't care about that. All they want is results. So, here's the plan. Ready?"

Rubbing her hands together she said, "Just say the word. Oh, before I forget, thanks for accepting me as your partner."

They looked into one another's eyes for a brief moment before Greg reluctantly returned his gaze to the road.

Kate felt a surge of longing for the tall, good-looking man at her side, but quickly tamped it down. The people she was involved with ran through her mind and knew she would never attempt to drag Greg down with her no matter how attractive she found him.

Unaware of her inner turmoil, Greg favored her with a winning smile, and then glanced quickly at the length of shapely leg revealed under the pink skirt.

"You're welcome. Are you married, Kate?" he asked realizing he knew nothing beyond the superficial about her.

Ignoring the invitation behind the smile, she shook her head. Keep it light, Kate, she told herself. "Nope, are you?"

"Nope are you dating anyone seriously?" he asked.

"Nope, are you?" She blinked several times to hold back tears that threatened to overflow at the unfairness of it all.

Not associating the sudden sparkle in her dark eyes, Greg felt a glimmer of hope. "Nope," wiping imaginary sweat from his brow with the back of his hand, he smiled at her again. "Boy, I'm glad we got that out of the way," he chuckled.

"Yeah, me too," she said softly.

"Okay, serious now. There are two banks in Cleveland and one just outside the city limits. I want you to find out if Armstrong banked at any of them. If you're lucky and he did, get a search warrant for a copy of both his personal and business accounts. I want to know how much money passed through each account and when."

By this time, they reached the intersection of Highway 129 and Greg entered the southbound lane to take them back to town.

"And, what will you be doing?" Kate asked as she busily scribbled notes in a tiny pad she'd pulled from her purse.

"Put in a call to the Augusta Police Department. I want to fax that certificate so they can send someone out to the medical school to check it out. I think it will be a waste of time, but it needs to be done."

A few minutes later, Greg turned into the parking lot where he parked as far away from the other cars as possible—he hated the idea of a ding in one of the Mustang's doors because of someone else's carelessness.

"Then I'm going down there" Exiting the car, he turned and headed for the building.

Hastily climbing from the car, Kate ran to catch up. "You're leaving me here alone? What if I'm asked something I can't answer? Or expected to do something I don't know how to do?"

Greg laughed as he held the door open for her. "Rookie, I find it hard to believe you'd be afraid of anything."

"Duh! Do you think it's wise handing me so much responsibility . . . on my first day?"

"What was it you said to me this morning? I don't need you to hold my hand? Besides, tomorrow will be your second day." Not waiting for a response, he turned and headed for his desk.

Flinging her purse over her shoulder, Kate caught up with him just as he dropped the stack of folders he'd been carrying atop the pile on his desk. "Don't tell me you plan to take everything I say literally."

Any response Greg may have given was cut off by the sudden appearance of

Boswell, who had rushed out of his office as soon as he saw them enter the room.

"Nesbit called. He has a preliminary autopsy report ready. He'll be out here in the morning to go over it with you."

"Great," Greg said with enthusiasm.

Boswell glanced at the clock on the back wall. "It's almost five. Why don't you two knock off for the day?"

Greg picked up a stack of messages from the desk before turning to Kate. "Well, Rookie. You did a great job on your first day."

She smiled but this one didn't even reach her eyes and Greg wondered if there was something on her mind or if she was simply tired from a long day. Just tired, he decided. "Thanks. So, are we calling it a day?"

Greg sank into the uncomfortable desk chair. "Go home, Kate. Get some rest. I'll fill the chief here in on our day."

Boswell waited until she was out of the room before speaking. "How'd your partner work out?"

"Fine."

Boswell drummed his short fingers on the desk. "Have you run across any clues that could shed some light on who may have murdered them?"

Greg propped his elbow on the arm of the chair, resting his chin in the palm of his hand. "My guess would be the girl in the hospital, whoever she is."

"What proof do you have?"

"Absolutely none yet, it's just a gut feeling."

"You can't arrest her on a gut feeling. Get some facts to back it up. What do you have planned for tomorrow, other than the meeting with Nesbit?"

Ignoring Boswell's question for the moment, Greg leaned back, clasping his hands together behind his head. "I can tell you one thing that is a fact. Armstrong wasn't a doctor."

"How do you know?"

"Kate and I found a few 'patient files' in his office."

"And?"

"Kate decided to call a few of them—funny thing, they'd never heard of Armstrong before his name was blasted all over the newspapers and television.

The addresses listed for the ones Kate talked to were made up and the other names and addresses are non-existent." He paused for a moment. "I can't figure out why he did that. Why make up phony patients and take the time to keep records on them?"

Digging through the new stack of paperwork on his desk, Greg found the certificate and handed it to Boswell.

"Here's the kicker. It's from the Medical College of Georgia, in Augusta."

Boswell looked at it. "What's so strange about that?"

"Don't you think it's strange for a plastic surgeon to have a single certificate from one school? You've been in doctor's offices before. They usually have diplomas and certificates all over the walls. Where'd this guy go to medical school, where'd he do his residency?"

"Don't you think you should go down there?"

"I'm calling Augusta P.D. in the morning, and then I'll fax the certificate so one of their guys can check it out. Then I'll head down there."

"Good plan. Go home, Greg. You look like you've been rode hard and put away wet."

Greg stood, yawned loudly and nodded. "That's where I'm headed right now."

Boswell watched as the detective turned, heading for the exit. "Garrison," he called after him. "Don't try to fit this crime around the girl. You get the facts." With a silent wave of his hand, Greg went out the door and across the parking lot to his car.

Stopping on the way for a quick dinner,

Greg finally arrived home around six-thirty, where, after unceremoniously dropping his briefcase onto the floor, he collapsed into his favorite recliner, flipping the lever to raise the footrest. Exhaling loudly, he relaxed into the softness of the chair and closed his eyes. The day was catching up with him.

He began to drift toward a much-deserved slumber, but suddenly jerked awake with a start as images of the Armstrong's bodies sprawled across their kitchen floor filled his head. Sighing, he reached for the remote and turned on the television. Tired as he was, he knew it might be a long time before he'd be able to get a good night of sleep maybe a long, long time.

Chapter Ten

Although he'd only slept a couple hours, Greg sat at his desk adding sugar and cream to his first cup of coffee by seven-thirty when Kate arrived and plopped down in the chair next to his desk. He noticed with approval that she was dressed in an outfit that would allow her more freedom of movement and be more comfortable in the long run than the pink skirt and jacket she'd worn yesterday. The dark blue, man-tailored shirt of some slinky looking fabric, probably silk, was tucked neatly into a pair of tailored black slacks and her feet were clad in a pair of low-heeled black boots—nice indeed, he thought as he looked at her over the rim of his coffee cup.

"How was your night?" she asked. He shrugged. "That good mine too, so . . . tell me something about you."

Taking another sip of the hot coffee, he looked at her quizzically. "Like what?"

She looked up at the ceiling for a moment, and then back at him, dark eyes sparkling. "Like, do you hunt or fish? What do you do to relax after a rough day?"

He smiled, sat the cup down on the desk and leaned back in his chair. "I don't hunt, but I do love to fish. I plant a small vegetable garden every year. I also work in my yard. I love to get my hands in the dirt, and I love baseball. In fact, I was at a game with a friend when I got the call about the Armstrongs.

"I have exercise equipment in my basement and I try to work out a little everyday. I like to run five or six miles a day, but since this case started, I haven't been. What about you? What do you like to do?"

She smiled like a Cheshire cat. "Oh, I like to do needlepoint. I'm also an amateur artist." And past party-girl extraordinaire, she thought to herself and her smile faltered for a second before she willed the thought from her mind. "I'm not the outdoorsy type at all."

What was that look, Greg wondered, but before he could ask, Paul Nesbit strolled into the office and he and Kate both rose hastily to their feet.

"You ready for this?" Greg asked her.

"I think so."

They followed Nesbit into an empty conference room and Greg's stomach churned as he watched Nesbit place a box of slides on the table and turn on the slide projector, but he put on a brave face, pulled out a chair and sat down. Kate seated herself next to him, looking at Nesbit expectantly.

"Somebody sure didn't like these people," Paul said, as he carefully arranged the slides in the projector. "I'll start with the woman."

He handed each of them a copy of the autopsy report. "When I analyzed her blood for chemicals, I found cocaine and alcohol." Neither detective offered a response so he continued. "Examination of the bodies quite clearly revealed the sequence of the gunshots."

With the click of a button, a picture of the woman lying on the autopsy table flashed onto the screen. "The first bullet entered the left shoulder." He stepped close to the screen and pointed.

"The shooter was about the same height as the victim and stood some distance away. If the shooter were taller, the bullet would have entered at a downward angle. If the shooter were shorter, the bullet would have entered at an upward angle. The bullet entered in a straight line. The blood patterns on the stove and wall confirms this.

"There was no powder residue. The bullet went through the shoulder joint and severed an artery. That, my friends, was enough to cause her bleed to death."

He pressed the button to change the image on the screen. "The second bullet entered the right shoulder. The victim was already on the floor when she was shot the second time—evident by the downward trajectory of the bullet.

"The shooter was standing directly over the victim by this time. The bullet entered right below the collarbone, tore through the thorax barely missing her lung, and continued on a downward path until it lodged in the hip joint where it fragmented."

He pressed the button a third time to bring up an image of the victim's lower the lower abdomen. "This was another downward shot. The shooter was close but not closes enough to leave a lot of powder residue. The bullet entered right above the pelvic bone, ruptured the bladder, passed through the uterus, and exited the body. The crime lab dug the bullet out of the floor—it came from a nine-millimeter."

Taking a deep breath, Paul pressed the button yet again, this time bringing up an image of the victim's head. "Somebody had an intense dislike for this woman but she was a fighter. As I said, the first shot would have caused her to bleed to death—either of the other two caused enough internal damage to kill her as well, but she was still alive when the fourth bullet tore open her skull."

Raising his thumb and index finger, he held them close to the side of his head. "The shooter held the gun just inches from her head—and bam! Fired."

The next picture was a close-up of the gunshot wound on the left side of Mrs. Armstrong's head. "The powder burns here tell me our shooter was right-handed and standing to the victim's left. Firing the weapon this close sheered off a piece of the skull bone covering the brain. I'm certain brain matter sprayed back onto the shooter." Finished at last, he turned to them and waited for questions.

Kate was the first to speak. "You don't think she was dead from the other shots? If not, was there any possibility she could have lived through this?"

"Oh, no, she was dying from the shoulder wound. The other bullets were fired out of hate or rage, or whatever name you want to put on it. When that final bullet penetrated her brain, she was still alive. The bullet severed the facial nerve, causing the mouth to contort toward the wound." Again, he waited for questions.

Greg sighed and squirmed in his chair, trying to find a more comfortable position. "At the crime scene, you said they were stabbed. Will you elaborate on that?"

Paul pressed the button again to bring up an image of the stab wounds to the woman's chest. "There are five stab wounds to her chest, mostly to the breast area. These wounds were made postmortem. There is no blood around the entry marks and the wounds didn't begin to close as they would have if she was still alive when she'd been stabbed."

He paused for a moment to allow for questions from the detectives. When none were forthcoming, he said. "Okay, let's move on to the male victim."

The first image was one of Armstrong's leg wound. "Upon examination of the body at the crime scene, I determined this was the first entry wound because of the trajectory of the bullet and the massive destruction of the leg itself—along with the amount of blood loss and the blood splatter pattern.

"Again, the shooter was close, but not closes enough to leave powder residue. The victim was shorter than the shooter and was standing when the bullet entered the kneecap destroying before ricocheting and splintering the bone just below the joint of the knee, causing the leg to collapse and taking our victim down to the floor. The impact caused the bone to fragment and protrude through the flesh. I'd say for at least a short period of time he lost consciousness."

Paul paused, rotating his head and shoulders to ease the tension building at the back of his neck, and then pressed the button to reveal a picture of the shoulder injury. "Upon examining the loss of blood around this wound and blood patterns at the scene, I concluded that this was the second injury.

"Once again, the shooter stood directly over the victim aiming downward to fire repeatedly into the body. Any one of the next three shots were enough to kill him." He turned to observe the two detectives, saw the horror on their faces and released they were not as fascinated by these as he was and picked up the pace a bit.

"I don't know what the shooter was thinking here or even if he was thinking at this point. This shot blew open the victim's stomach, continued down the intestinal tract, and exited through the rectum. We found the slug when we moved the body." He quickly moved on to the next picture.

"He was shot in the head in the same manner as the woman, except the shooter wasn't as close to him—no powder residue." Turning off the projector, Paul turned to face the two detectives.

Greg swallowed hard, wishing he'd waited for that first cup of coffee until <u>after</u> this meeting. He could feel it churning in his stomach as it attempted to climb its way back up and out. "My God, Paul, what kind of person or people are we dealing with?"

"I don't know. But I'll tell you one thing I sure wouldn't want to get on his bad side." Paul answered and turned to Kate, whose face was pale under the carefully applied makeup. "Are you all right?"

"I'll be okay," she said, covering her mouth.

"You want to wait outside?" Greg asked, pouring her a glass of water from the metal pitcher that he'd brought in earlier that morning.

She cleared her throat as she gratefully reached for the glass. "No, I won't run away from this. I don't know what these people did, but no one deserves to die in this manner." She took a tentative sip from the glass and when it stayed down, took another before sitting the glass down on the tabletop.

"Wasn't Armstrong stabbed too?" Greg questioned. "Did you also find traces of cocaine and alcohol in his blood?"

"He was stabbed five times—four wounds in the chest area and one in the groin. But, I didn't find any drugs in his body."

"Didn't I hear you say they were shot with a nine-millimeter?" Greg asked.

"I have several good slugs. If you can locate the gun, I can easily make a positive match."

Greg rose to his feet. "Thanks for sharing those graphic visuals with us, Paul. I, for one, couldn't take much more. How about it, Kate? Have you seen enough?"

She rose too "more than enough."

The trio stepped into the hallway where Greg and Kate both let out loud sighs of relief. "Do you have any leads yet?" Paul asked.

"Nah at least no proof anyway," Greg answered as he escorted Paul to the front of the building. "Thanks again, Paul. Give me a call when the fiber results come in."

"It's going to be a while before those results come back. Possibly two or three months—they're so backlogged it's not funny." He pulled a set of keys from his pocket and turned toward his car.

"I don't suppose you could put a rush on it, could you?"

Paul turned to him with a chuckle. "Stand in line, pal. That's what everyone else wants too. All I can tell you is that when they're finished, we'll get the report. Talk to you later." He crossed the half-full parking lot, unlocked his car, clambered in and drove away without a backward glance.

Boswell emerged from his office to join Greg as he returned to his desk. "What did you find out from Paul?"

"They're still dead."

"I know that," Boswell said, taking a

seat.

Greg ran his fingers through his hair. "The woman had cocaine in her blood but the husband was clean. But we're no closer to finding out why they were murdered than we were on the day it happened." <u>Why can't I get a feeling for this? Why can't I put my finger on something</u>, he wondered for the thousandth time.

"Greg, it's only the fifth day. Something will turn up."

"Thanks Boss. But you know as well as I do that the first twenty-four hours after a murder is critical—and that time frame is fading further and further into the past."

Boswell was silent for a moment, and then exhaled slowly. "I got a call from the District Attorney this morning. He wants me in his office this afternoon to present a progress report."

Greg looked at him curiously. "What will you tell him?"

"Tell me what your agenda is for the day and that's what I'll tell Clayton." He stood, giving Greg's shoulder a reassuring pat. "Aaah—don't worry about Clayton. He just wants to get in front of the television camera and look pretty. He wouldn't know how to solve a crime if he had directions, but he really wants to get elected for a second term and bringing this case to trial might just do it for him."

Glancing around to see who was in earshot, he lowered his voice before confiding, "I didn't vote for him the first time and I won't this time either. You worry about the case and let me worry about Thomas Clayton." He winked lewdly, which made Greg guffaw, and then returned to the privacy of his office.

As Greg reread his notes from the past several days, Kate approached. "I just talked wit a rep at the phone company who confirmed that Langston placed a disconnect order on Sunday—service to be discontinued Monday morning."

"I can't figure that out. Why did she leave town?"

Kate shrugged. "Maybe she was afraid whoever killed the Armstrong's would come after her next."

"Or maybe she's an accomplice."

Kate groaned. "Are you still trying to pin this on the girl in the hospital?"

Tossing the pencil on the desk, Greg nodded. "Give me another suspect and I'll be happy to consider him."

"You're like a pit bull. You sink your teeth into something and refuse to let go."

"Sit, Kate. Let's go over what we already know. Fact number one, someone murdered the Armstrong's. Fact number two, there was no forced entry and no fingerprints except for those belonging to the Armstrong's and Bethany Akin.

"Are we in agreement so far?" At her nod, he continued. "Good. Now here's what we don't have at this point—a motive and the murder weapons. Who removed them from the scene?"

Kate shrugged. "But that's still no reason to blame Bethany Akin. Maybe the victims knew their assailant. And gloves could explain the lack of prints. Unless the killer had completely lost it before he finished, there's no way he'd leave the weapons behind. I sure wouldn't. Would you?"

Ignoring the question, Greg moved on. "What about the phony files? Explain why Miss Langston left town so suddenly. And here's another thing—if she were afraid the killer would come after her why didn't she say something on Saturday night? Remember, she came here looking for me. I didn't go looking for her. I didn't even know she existed."

Kate shrugged again. "I don't know. Maybe she was afraid the cops in a small town like this couldn't protect her."

Greg pounded his fist on the desk in anger. "Bull! She lived here for ten years.

She knew exactly what we could do. In fact, I'd bet she was counting on it. Looking back on it, I think that's why she came to see me in the first place—she wanted to know what I'd found out. After talking to me, she knew she still had time to make a clean getaway."

Kate laughed derisively. "That's supposition, where's your proof?"

Greg tossed his notepad on his desk. "I don't have any yet. But I will."

"Sure you will. You're not one of those detective's who fabricate evidence just to be right, are you?"

The look he gave her would have sent a lesser woman running for cover. "Rookie, you don't know me. If I'm wrong about this girl, I'll be the first to say so. But right now, there's no other suspect. If you think I'm wrong, prove it."

Kate was embarrassed. "I'm sorry. You're right, I don't know you."

"Forget it. So you're visiting the banks this morning and I'm calling Augusta, right?"

"I'm leaving right now."

Greg turned in his chair to watch her leave then called the front desk to get the number for the Police Department in Augusta. Thanking the officer for the information, he disconnected the call, and then dialed the number.

"Good morning, this is Detective Greg Garrison in Cleveland, Georgia. May I speak with a detective?"

After a short pause, a big voice, seeming to belong to a big man boomed into his ear. "This is Lieutenant Ralph Harkins. How can I help you, Detective Garrison?"

"I'm sure you've already heard, but we had a double homicide here last Saturday— Doctor Joseph Armstrong and his wife, Bette, were murdered in their home.

"When my partner and I checked out his office yesterday, we found a certificate from the Medical College of Georgia. I'd like to fax the certificate to you, along with his fingerprints and a photograph so you can check your files to see if you have any record of arrests or traffic violations on him. Could you help me?"

"Yeah, we've discussed the case a few times. Sounds pretty gruesome I'd be glad to help in any way I can. Do you have our fax number?"

"No."

"It's 404-555-3785. Send everything to my attention—Lieutenant Ralph Harkins."

"Thanks, Ralph. I plan to be down your way tomorrow."

"Look forward to it."

Chief Boswell stormed out of his office as Greg hung up the phone. "I just got off the phone with Hargrove. The girl is ready to tell us what she knows."

Greg was busy writing the message and gathering what he wanted to fax to Harkins. "Not yet. I want to know more about her parents before I talk to her."

"Kate's gone to check with the banks in town to see where Armstrong did business. When she finds out, we'll get a warrant for copies of everything. I'm leaving for Augusta in the morning."

"You think she can handle things while you're gone?"

"She's very competent,"

Boswell pointed a finger at Greg. "Just remember, I'm holding you responsible for everything she does—right or wrong."

Greg opened his mouth to respond, but was interrupted by the ringing telephone. "Garrison here oh hi, Kate. Great! Now go see Judge Nobel about the warrant. See you later." He hung up the phone, and without looking at Boswell, said, "Competent."

"Good. So what did she find?"

"I'm sorry my mind is running in fifteen different directions at once. She found the bank the Armstrong's used—White County Bank and Trust. That's the one on the outskirts of town.

"You heard me tell her to go see Judge

Nobel. We should have the records by the time I return from Augusta." The chief nodded as Greg gathered his paperwork and headed for the fax machine.

Chapter Eleven

Bethany Akin's long, chestnut hair was pulled in a ponytail and she sat quietly in the Queen Anne's chair in front of Dr. Hargrove's desk. Her unusual eyes had regained their sparkle and her peaches and cream complexion glowed with good health. Dressed in jeans and a short-sleeved white pullover, she looked much different than the confused young woman who'd been brought in with blood in her hair and some unseen terror pursuing her at every turn.

Thinking about his own daughters for a moment, Dr. Hargrove smiled across the desk at her. "Are you ready to talk about what happened?"

Rising gracefully, she crossed the room to look out the window. "Is it hot outside?"

"Yes, it's June and it's very hot." Dr. Hargrove joined her. "Tell me what happened," he prompted.

Feeling a sudden chill, which made her shiver, she turned to him. "I didn't kill them."

He motioned for her to sit down again and when she complied, he responded. "I believe you, Bethany. But it's not me that you have to convince. It's Lieutenant Garrison, who is heading up the investigation that you'll have to explain everything to."

"Does he have any idea who did this?"

"Not yet. He is hoping you can help him find out what happened."

She raised her hands in a shrug, and then let them flop back into her lap. "I'm so afraid. I don't know who to trust."

"I believe Lieutenant Garrison can be trusted to do the right thing."

Closing her medical file, which he had been perusing when she came into the room, he returned to the desk and sat down again. "It is not my job to accuse you of anything––I simply want to help you get through this. But, you've got to understand that this is a capital crime. The police will look at everyone who knew the Armstrong's, including you."

"But I <u>didn't</u> know them. I was only trying to find my sister. They were the only link I had so I wouldn't want to kill them. I needed them"

"When the police finish their investigation, I'm sure you will be exonerated."

She wiped tears from her face with the back of her hand. "I just wish I knew where my sister was—please, you must believe that I didn't kill anyone. I couldn't."

"Bethany, if you tell Lieutenant Garrison exactly what you saw inside the house, I'm sure he'll believe you."

She was silent for a moment and then looked past him to something unseen. "He has to believe me because I'm innocent."

Chapter Twelve

Thursday morning, Greg was up at five-thirty, freshly showered, shaved, and dressed for the trip to Augusta. The kitchen smelled of fresh coffee and he inhaled deeply as he filled his travel mug, turned off the coffee maker and went out the door.

The drive was uneventful but as the miles floated past and the sun began to rise further into the sky, he could feel its heat through the tinted windows as it attempted to turn the interior of the Mustang into an oven despite the valiant efforts of the air-conditioner. By the time he trotted across the parking lot from the car to the building his recently clean shirt was plastered to his back with sweat and he grumbled under his breath, "Damn, this heat."

Once inside, he identified himself and asked for Ralph Harkins—who, when he appeared, was as big as Greg had imagined when they'd spoken on the phone yesterday. At least as tall as he was, Harkins had fifty pounds on Greg but none of it was fat. The guy was pure muscle and Greg, ever the football fan, could easily envision him as a linebacker on a winning team. The man's dark skin was beaded with sweat and the beefy hand he extended to Greg was damp despite his effort to wipe it off on a pant leg first.

"Sorry about that. Once the hot weather hits, I can't seem to cool down no matter what I do. How's the investigation coming along?" he asked as he led the way to his desk

"That depends on what you found out for me."

Pulling an extra chair up to the desk for Greg, Ralph squeezed his too-large frame into another chair before responding. "I went over to the Medical College yesterday. Just as you suspected there was no record of Joseph Armstrong ever being a student there."

"Did you find any records on him

here?"

Harkins pulled an arrest folder out from a small, neat stack on his desk—<u>nothing at all like my clutter</u> Greg thought as he watched him easily locate the information. "Since he's been in Cleveland for the last ten years, I began a search of our data files at 1987, working my way back to 1980." Flipping open the folder, he pulled out a few photos and spread them on the desk in front of Greg.

"Look here. Granted, this guy has a different name, but for some reason he seems to have Armstrong's face—right down to an identical scar beginning over the left eyebrow and extending down the cheek." His finger traced the mark on the picture as he spoke.

"May I?" Greg asked and at Harkins' nod, he pulled a rap sheet from the folder and began reading. "Philip Sharply from Quincy, Massachusetts, arrested on possession and distribution of a controlled substance. How did he get off?"

Ralph handed Greg another folder. "Sharply was arrested in 1985 for selling cocaine to an undercover officer. His lawyer, Emmett Fuller—now there's a name synonymous with the drug world, got the charges dismissed because some of the evidence was misplaced or lost. There was a little bit of a mystery as to how the stuff simply disappeared but with no evidence there wasn't much to hold Sharply with.

"Case closed, information stuck in a computer until needed. I know the guy who arrested him. He's retired now but I could talk to him to see if he remembers anything. Seems like a pretty routine arrest but maybe something stuck in his head. You never know."

"Where's the lawyer?"

"Dead got killed in a head-on collision about three years ago."

Greg tossed the folder back on the table. "Heaven forbid that I'd get just one break.

Oh well, what about Armstrong's fingerprints? Did you verify that Sharply and Armstrong are the same person?"

Harkins rose, a broad smile on his ebony face. "Come on, I'll introduce you to the smartest computer person in the state. In fact, he's so smart the Georgia Bureau of Investigation keeps trying to steal him away from us. You know how those hounds are—get a scent of something they like and you can't get 'em to back off no matter what."

The two men laughed as they entered the elevator and rode up one floor. It was no secret that local police departments thought the GBI consisted of a bunch of morons who made a practice of looking for real talent outside the hallways of their department.

As they exited the elevator, Harkins called out to a young Asian man who was entering the other elevator. "Wait up a minute, Saung Hai. I have someone here I want you to meet."

Hai stepped from the elevator just before the door shut and smiled up at Harkins. "Hi, Ralph."

"This is Detective Greg Garrison with the White Sheriff's Department in Cleveland." He continued without waiting for the two men to acknowledge one another. "Have you finished with the fingerprints I gave to you yesterday?"

"It takes a while and I'm in the middle of another project, but I'll be finished in about an hour. How long can you wait?"

"As long as it takes," Greg answered.

"Good," Hai nodded. "Can you come back in the morning around nine-thirty or ten o'clock? I should have something for you by then."

"Great. See you then. And, thanks," Greg said extending his hand, which Hai promptly shook.

The two detectives returned to the elevator, and then Harkins escorted Greg outside into the searing June heat. "My God, man, how do you all stand this heat?" Greg asked as he stripped off his sports coat and folded it over his arm.

Ralph laughed. "You think its hot now? Come back down here at the end of July or any time in August. That's when it's hot."

"If you don't mind, I'll just take your word for it. Can you recommend a halfway decent place to stay that's fairly close by?" They had reached his car and Greg opened the door and an almost visible cloud of stuffy, over-heated air rolled out at them.

"There's a La Quinta Inn a couple of blocks south of here. You can't miss it," Harkins said, pointing down the street.

"Thanks. I'll see you tomorrow." He gingerly climbed behind the wheel, started the car and turned the air-conditioner up as high as it would go. He could hear Harkins' laughter as the big man offered a wave over his shoulder as he hurried back to the relative coolness of the building, and then he slammed the door and drove away.

Chapter Thirteen

When Greg returned to police headquarters the next morning, Harkins was waiting for him just inside the door. "Let's go see that computer guy work his magic," he said by way of greeting, and then took Greg back upstairs to the coolest part of the building—the computer room.

"Morning, Saung. We're here to observe the master do that thing he does so well." Saung smiled and the two detectives took positions behind him where they could watch the blue screen he'd been monitoring when they came in.

"I made a hard copy of both sets of fingerprints," Saung explained as they waited. "After marking the sections of each set of fingerprints that are unique to each person, I scanned both sets into the computer this morning.

"Sharply is on the left, Armstrong on the right. I'll merge the prints, and—" He paused as he pressed a few keys, and then looked back at the monitor. "The computer will check to see if the markings I made match.

"If they do, then we'll know Sharply and Armstrong are the same man. If not . . ." he shrugged. "It will tell us either way."

Greg watched the computer screen, fascinated, as the two sets of prints merged into one. "Is it a match?"

"Don't know yet. The computer is still working."

In the next instant, the word 'MATCH' flashed onto the computer screen. Shaking his head in disbelief, Greg swore softly under his breath. "I'll be damned!"

Harkins crowed triumphantly, slapped Greg on the back so hard he almost lost his balance and held up a hand for Saung to give him a high-five. All three men were smiling. "There's your answer. Armstrong is Sharply fingerprints don't lie."

"I'll print a copy for your files," Saung said as he pushed a few more keys, and then turned to remove the page as it emerged from the printer.

Still smiling, Greg shook Saung's hand, then Harkins' hand, and then Saung's again. "It's been a real pleasure working with you two and I appreciate your help. And now I need to head back home." Shaking hands all around one final time, Greg returned to his car and left Cleveland.

By early afternoon, Greg hurried into the Cleveland police station where Boswell immediately called him into his office. "The reports on the bullets came back from the State Crime Lab—no luck there.

"Someone had the foresight to send them on to the FBI and we got a report back this morning. We have a perfect match to an unsolved murder in Quincy, Massachusetts. The victim's name was Bennie J. Trotter."

This is turning into a good day, Greg thought, smiling—no, a great day. "I have some news of my own. I got the fingerprint results on Armstrong—those guys in Augusta are really good; Joseph Armstrong's real name is Philip Sharply."

"Uh huh and what does that have to do with anything at this point?"

By this time, Greg was grinning from ear to ear. "Before he came to Georgia to become Joseph Armstrong, our victim lived in Quincy as Philip Sharply." The look on Boswell's face was so priceless that Greg found himself wishing for a camera to record the moment for posterity.

"Wow. So, I guess you're planning another trip, huh?"

Shaking his head, Greg explained his reasoning. "I will, but not just yet. I want to get in touch with the Athens Police Department and ask them to pay a little visit to Brenda Armstrong. I'm really curious as to why she hasn't shown up yet.

"Then, I want to get a court order for her phone records. I want to know who she's called and who's called her. If my luck holds, we'll find out that she's spoken with someone in Quincy recently."

"What's whirling around in that brain of yours?"

Greg paced the length of the room, and then stopped in front of Boswell's desk. "I have a feeling that Armstrong was hiding from somebody and they found him. I don't think he contacted anyone in Quincy, but maybe his daughter did, not realizing that by doing so she put her parents in jeopardy. That's why I need those telephone records."

"That sounds logical. Kate's dad is the Chief of Police in Athens. Do you think she should call him?"

"No. I'll take care of it right now. That is, if we're through?"

Boswell waved him out. "Go. It's about time we got a break in this case. By the way, what is Kate working on?"

"I told you, Chief. She found the Armstrong's bank and the last thing I heard she was waiting on the court order to subpoena the records."

At his desk, Greg called the Clarke County Police Department. After several rings, a woman, identifying herself as Sergeant Perkins answered. Greg told her who he was, briefly explained the case and asked to speak with Chief O'Connor.

"Good morning, Lieutenant, what can I do for you?"

"Good morning, sir. Thank you for taking my call. I'm sure you're fully aware of the double homicide we had up here a few days ago."

"Yes, it's been all over the news. What can I do to help?"

"Funny you should ask because that's the reason for my call. The daughter of the deceased couple, Brenda Armstrong, is a student at the University of Georgia. Could you find out where she lives and get one of your detectives to pay her a visit? I also need a court order for her phone records. "

"Consider it done."

"How long do you think it will take?"

"Not long at all. I'll go see Judge Hart just as soon as I get off the phone. We should have a copy of her phone records by this afternoon. By the way, Lieutenant, how's my little girl working out?"

"Kate's doing a great job. In fact, she's working with me on this case."

"Glad to hear that. Give me a few hours I should know something by then."

As Greg reviewed notes and skimmed over the case file, Kate arrived, carrying two large folders, which she dropped onto the top of her desk.

"Hi," she said with a smile. "It's good to see you back." She pointed at the folders to make sure he'd seen them. "See this stuff? It's the business and personal banking records of the Armstrong's." She crossed the room to pour a cup of coffee then returned to her desk, asked him if he was ready to start reviewing the material.

As he wheeled his chair toward her desk, Kate lifted the cup to sip at the hot liquid, spilling some of it across the back of her hand.

"You look a little shaky there, Kate," Greg said as he pulled a wad of tissue from a box on the corner of her desk and passed it to her, "everything okay?"

Sitting the cup down, she took the tissue and dabbed at her hand before raising it to her lips for a moment, "yeah, sure. Everything's fine."

He stared at her for a moment, noticing the dark circles under her eyes, the faint lines of exhaustion around her mouth, but decided not to pursue it. If she said she was okay, then she was okay.

"Which one is the business account?"

"The one on the bottom, but you're not going to find his signature on anything." She flipped open the top folder to show him the signature card.

"Beatrice Langston was the only person authorized to sign anything, including checks. In fact, Joseph Armstrong's name doesn't appear anywhere except at the top of his personal checks—along with his wife's name and Miss Langston's."

Greg examined the signature card before picking up a copy of a cancelled check from the personal account file. "Did they say why?"

"Nope. They were his accounts and if that's the way he wanted to handle things, it was fine with the bank. I also found out that they had a safe deposit box, but my paperwork didn't cover it so the manager wouldn't let me touch it."

Tossing the signature card aside, Greg flipped open the business account folder. "Wait a minute. Langston told me that Armstrong was a plastic surgeon, but the name of the company on these checks is Cleveland Surgical Consultants. Why did she lie?"

Holding up a hand to delay any response Kate might have offered, he chuckled at his own stupidity. "Listen to me! Of course she's going to lie! Armstrong wasn't a doctor or a consultant. As a matter of fact, his name wasn't even Joseph Armstrong because he was Philip Sharply from Quincy, Massachusetts."

"Where did that little tidbit come from?"

"Augusta. I met a great guy down there who checked old files to see if anyone matching Armstrong's description came up. And sure enough, someone did—Philip Sharply. We checked both sets of fingerprints and got a perfect match."

She stared at him, wide eyed. "Good job, Greg."

"Yeah, but it's just one small piece of a great big puzzle. Let's get back to the problem at hand. You go over the personal account and I'll take the business account to my desk. Once we've gone through both of them we'll compare notes. Okay?"

She nodded and he returned to his desk where he tried to concentrate on the task at

hand instead of thinking about Kate—
something didn't seem quite right about her,
but he couldn't put his finger on it and it was
driving him up the wall. His cop's intuition
told him she was in trouble but he knew
better than to pry—he'd simply have to wait
until she was ready to volunteer information
about what was bothering her. Until then, he
needed to pay attention to what he was
doing. It wouldn't help anything if he
overlooked pertinent information because he
was worried about his partner's private life.

As he pulled the account activity
printout from the folder to see how much
money had been processed, he let out a low
whistle. "Wow!" He began to look at the
deposit history and quickly ascertained that
large sums of money were deposited in this
account only to be transferred to an account
outside of the country within a few days.
The deposits grew in size and became more
numerous with each passing year. The week
of the murders, seven deposits, totaling well
over ten million dollars, were made.

The pattern up until that point had been
money deposited on Friday, wire transfers
on the following Monday—until the last
week where everything changed. The final
transfer had been made Saturday morning—
the day of the murders, and everything had
gone to a new account in the Caribbean.
Immediately following verification of the
transfer, the account in Cleveland was
closed.

Laying the printouts aside, Greg dug
through the folder to find the required
authorization slip needed to make the
transfer, and then he grabbed the signature
card. Even for a layman, it was evident that
Langston had signed both. It also looked like
her hand might have been shaking a bit
when she made that last transfer. Gee, I
wonder what she had to be nervous about,
Greg thought.

It was possible that someone had forced
her to transfer the money, but if that was

true, why hadn't she said anything when she talked to him on Saturday night. Could Langston be the killer? Were the Armstrong's murdered because of her greed, her desires to have what wasn't hers and probably never would be unless she stole it?

Stuffing everything back into the folder, Greg stood and headed for Boswell's office. "Be right back, Kate." Acknowledging him with a wave of her hand, she didn't look up from the papers spread out in front of her.

After sharing his discovery with his boss, Greg told him that he wanted to go see Judge Noble "To get a search warrant for the Armstrong's safe deposit box."

"Are you taking Kate with you?"

Greg looked through the open doorway at Kate who absently rubbed at her stomach as if it ached. "No. She's pretty wrapped up in the bank files. I shouldn't be too long."

Turning away from her, Greg exhaled heavily. "Boss, I've got a real bad feeling about this case. I'm almost afraid of what I'll find next."

Boswell got up and placed a hand on Greg's shoulder. "You're a good cop, Greg. Cleveland may be a little town—a speck of fly shit on a map of the world, so to speak. But, we still have laws and someone committed a murder here."

"Now the way I see it, we have two choices. We can back off because we're scared of what we might find and call in the GBI boys—you know they're itching to get a hold of this case. Or, we can move forward and try to solve it. No matter what we find or who we implicate."

"No, I don't want to back off. It's my case and no matter how difficult it gets, I'll do my job."

Boswell nodded his approval. "That's what I want to hear. You find clues, gather your evidence and follow your leads carefully and thoroughly. And remember there's no such thing as a perfect murder, just bad police work.

"We're being watched by everyone—the GBI and the FBI, who are just waiting for us to fall on our butts so they can gloat about how small towns don't have the intelligence or experience to solve their own crimes. I want to solve this so we can rub their noses in it, don't you?"

"Chief, I never said I couldn't solve this case. I know I can. But, when I get one of these gut feelings it scares the hell out of me. I can't help it. I think Armstrong was laundering drug money right here under our noses—not much else I can think of that would generate that kind of money. I want to know who he was working for.

"Does this mean the drug lords think we're such a small town that they can come in here and run their business without us being any the wiser?" He turned again to glance at Kate, who was still thumbing through the bank account file and taking notes. "What about Kate? I don't want her to get hurt."

"Whoa, Greg you're way out of line there. She's a police office just like you. She knew the risks involved when she took the job so don't even start with that protect the woman crap." Greg opened his mouth to protest, but Boswell cut him off. "No. And I mean no. You do your job and Kate will do hers. End of discussion.

"Now, get on to the bank and see what's what. Then check back in with me."

Chapter Fourteen

The tie worn by Mr. Bigalow, the bank's branch manager, appeared to be knotted much too tightly as his neck bulged above the knot and his red face turned even redder when Greg handed him the authorization slip and asked him to identify the teller who had conducted the transaction. His reedy, little voice pricked at Greg's nerves when he picked up the phone and dialed an extension.

"Cathy," he said to the woman on the other end. "Would you come into my office?"

A moment later, a young woman who was so thin Greg thought she must surely be anorexic joined them. Bigalow motioned for her to sit and she scurried like a little mouse to the chair, where she sat, hands tightly clasped in her lap.

Handing her the slip of paper, Bigalow asked, "Aren't these your initials?"

"Yes, sir" she looked nervously from one man to the other. "Is there a problem?"

"Good question, Cathy, but I'm not sure. This is Detective Garrison and he's the one who wants to know."

As he pulled out his notepad and flipped to a clean page, Greg couldn't help but compare this scrawny little woman to Kate who was everything this woman wasn't— tall, slender, beautiful . . . Stop it, he told himself firmly. You seem to have Kate on the brain today. Be professional, man. Do your job. "What's your full name, Miss?"

"Cathy Gentry" she answered

Greg pointed to the piece of paper she still held. "Miss Gentry—it is Miss, isn't it?" At her nod, he continued. "Do you remember helping Miss Langston last Saturday?"

She stared blankly at the piece of paper for a second, and then snapped her fingers. "Yes, I remember now. She came in shortly after we opened. My window just happened to be the only empty one so there she was."

She pursed her lips at him and it took Greg a moment to realize it was her attempt at a smile.

Odd, he thought, but continued, "and?"

"She told me she wanted to transfer all the money from the business account. So I gave her a transfer slip. When she was finished, I did as she requested."

Mr. Bigalow leaned forward. "So, is there a problem?"

"Is it normal for one of your tellers to transfer that much money without your authorization?"

"Well, not just any teller can do that. But Miss Gentry . . ." he paused, glancing at the young woman, giving her a quick wink. She stared back, wide-eyed. So that's the way it is, Greg thought as he caught the little exchange. "Miss Gentry," Bigalow continued, "Is our head teller and I have every confidence in her judgment."

"Uh huh did you know that the Armstrong's were being murdered at almost the exact moment this transaction took place?"

"No, of course not, how would I know that? We . . . I heard about the murder on the radio sometime later that day."

Choosing to ignore the little slip, Greg turned to Miss Gentry. "When you heard about the murders, did it ever cross your mind that you should call the police?"

"Why, because of this transaction?"

Greg nodded, "yeah, because of that transaction. How many times had Miss Langston come in to request a transfer of funds like this?"

Clearing his throat, Bigalow smiled at Greg. "I think I can clear this up for you, Detective. The Armstrong business account was merely a holding account. There was no activity other than the deposits on Fridays, followed by the transfer of funds to the master account on Mondays."

Greg smiled back at him. "But that's not what happened on Saturday, is it?"

"No, but we had no reason to be suspicious of transferring the money a few days early. Miss Langston was the one always doing the transfers so there was absolutely no reason for alarm."

"Was Miss Langston alone Saturday morning?"

Cathy closed her eyes tightly in concentration for a moment, and then shook her head. "No. There was a man with her."

"Can you describe him?"

She looked at her boss who nodded. "He was about five foot six with perfect little white teeth—I noticed them because he kept smiling at me. But it was one of those smiles that never made it all the way to his pale blue eyes. You know what I mean?"

When Greg nodded his understanding, she continued. "He had really pink cheeks, almost as if he was wearing blusher, but I think it was natural.

"I remember his hands because he had the most perfectly manicured nails I've ever seen on a man. He just seemed so . . . I don't know. So pampered, I guess."

"And had this pampered little man ever come in with Miss Langston before?"

Cathy shrugged. "I really don't know. I wasn't the only one who waited on her, but I'd never seen him before."

"Did either of you ever see this man with Mr. Armstrong?"

Bigalow squirmed in his chair, and although Greg would have thought it was impossible, his face turned even redder. "None of us have ever met Mr. Armstrong, Detective."

Greg raised his eyebrows, leaning forward in his chair. "You mean to tell me the guy had two accounts worth millions of dollars in this bank, and no one here knew him? How can that be? Surely you met him when he first opened the accounts."

"I can see where this might be confusing. But, the previous bank president, Mr. Ogden, handled all of that. Five years ago, he contracted cancer and retired—he died six months later. As far as I know, he was the only one here who ever met Mr. Armstrong or his wife in person."

Greg stood abruptly, withdrew the warrant from his jacket pocket and passed it across the desk to Mr. Bigalow. "This is for the safe deposit box and its contents."

"Everything seems to be in order," he said after a moment. "I'll bring it to you."

Greg held up a hand to stop him. "I don't think so. I think I'll come with you."

After Mr. Bigalow unlocked the safe deposit box, he left Greg alone in the room. Glancing around to make sure he was alone, Greg opened the box.

Inside was a stack of one-hundred-dollar bills bundled fifty-thousand to a stack with ten stacks in all. Tucked underneath the stacks of money he discovered two life insurance policies—one on Armstrong for one and a half million dollars, and one on his wife in the amount of eight hundred thousand dollars. Brenda Armstrong was listed as the beneficiary on both. What a surprise, Greg thought as he placed the contents of the box into his briefcase and called for Bigalow, who reluctantly issued him a receipt. He thanked the bank manager and his "head cashier," winking at the woman who blushed in confusion, and smiling at Bigalow, who scowled in return. Greg began to whistle to himself as he sauntered out of the bank, briefcase locked securely to his wrist with a pair of handcuffs.

Chief Boswell came out of his office just as Greg arrived at his desk. "What was in the box?"

The phone rang. "Detective Garrison," Greg answered.

"Lieutenant, this is Chief O'Connor. I have those phone records you wanted."

"Already?"

"I requested a printout from the first of this year. Do you want to make a trip over here, or should I fax them? Quite a few pages here, by the way, no one answered the door at her apartment and she hasn't been attending classes either."

"Do me a favor and look to see if she made any calls to a place called Quincy, Massachusetts."

Papers rustled before O'Connor came back on the line. "Yes. There were several calls made to 541-555-6787."

Greg hurriedly wrote the number down. "Thanks, Chief. I'd appreciate if you'd fax everything to me."

"You're quite welcome. If there's anything else I can do, let me know. If that's it for now, is my little girl available?"

"Sure, hold on. Kate, your dad's on line four." She looked up in surprise, but reached for the phone as Greg motioned for Chief Boswell to go into his office where he closed the door behind them and drew the blinds across the windows.

"This is what was in the safe deposit box," he said, opening the briefcase on Boswell's desk. "There's five hundred thousand dollars here in crisp, new, five hundred dollar bills, neatly bundled in stacks of one thousand."

Boswell's jaw dropped as he stared at Greg in disbelief, "holy shit that's half a million dollars!"

"That's right. We need to walk it through the evidence room to be checked in and out so it can be deposited into the special account at the bank."

Boswell nodded as he reverently touched a stack of the money. He smiled at Greg and shook his head. "I've never seen this much money before."

Greg pulled out the insurance policies. "Two life insurance policies" he explained. "One on Joseph Armstrong in the amount of one and a half million dollars and one on his wife in the amount of eight hundred thousand dollars. I'll give you three guesses as to who the beneficiary is. And I won't even count the first two."

"The daughter?"

"Damn, you're good. With mommy and daddy dead, Brenda becomes an instant millionaire, which certainly gives her motive. Now we just need to come up with the means and opportunity. One small hitch though."

"What's that?"

"O'Connor sent someone to her apartment and she wasn't there—no one's seen her at school either."

"Hmm so what about the girl in the hospital, don't you want to talk to her too?"

"Yes, but not yet. First, I want to know who Brenda talked to in Quincy. Maybe she's up there. Hey, if you don't mind, I'd like you to take this money down to the evidence room." He undid the handcuffs and passed the briefcase to Boswell, who shook his head.

"No way, you're the one who located it. We'll walk it through together and then head over to the bank. I'll have a couple of uniformed officers follow us in their car," Boswell said as he pushed the briefcase back to Greg, who didn't protest.

"It's Friday. Do you want to leave for Quincy today or wait until Monday?" Boswell asked, changing the subject.

"I think I'll wait until Monday," Greg said. And for some reason his thoughts turned to Kate once more.

Chapter Fifteen

The flight was uneventful—the plane landed in Boston, Massachusetts at three o'clock on Monday afternoon where Greg rented a car, drove to Quincy, and got a room at the Ramada Inn. It was five-thirty by the time he placed a call to the phone number he'd gotten from Chief O'Connor. After several rings a woman answered.

"Who am I speaking to, please?"

"Who do you want to speak to?"

"My name is Detective Greg Garrison. I'm with the Cleveland, Georgia Sheriff's Department and I'm calling to see if you, or someone in your household, know a young woman named Brenda Armstrong?"

"Hold on a minute." A moment later a man picked up the phone. Greg repeated his request.

"She's my niece," the man answered after a short pause.

"Are you related to Joseph and Bette Armstrong?"

"No."

"What about Philip Sharply?"

"No."

Greg shook his head in frustration and tossed his pen down onto the table. "I'm afraid I don't understand. How can you be her uncle?"

There was a longer pause this time, followed by a long sigh. "Her name isn't Brenda Armstrong. It's Tammy Cutler. Her birth father was my brother."

Greg was silent for a moment as he digested this new piece of information. "Did you know the Armstrong's were murdered?"

The man cleared his throat. "Yes, I heard."

Greg picked up his pen again, ready to write down any important information the man might provide. "So, you _did_ know the Armstrong's?"

"No. But I knew Philip Sharply. He murdered my brother with a car bomb twenty years ago."

"I'm sorry, sir. I didn't get your name."

"George Cutler."

"Mr. Cutler, would it be possible for us to meet? I think it might be easier to discuss this in person."

"If you're really who you say you are I'll sit down at my kitchen table with you in the morning. But I want a badge number now and I want a phone number to the Sheriff's Department where you work so I can call and verify it."

"I understand your caution, Mr. Cutler." Greg provided him with the requested information and George Cutler promised to call him back within thirty minutes if he was satisfied with what he learned. He was and provided Greg with directions to his home.

The house nestled snugly between two others at the end of the street it was fair-sized white stucco. Small clusters of wildflowers bloomed along the edges of the brick walkway and a tall, slender spruce shaded the front lawn.

Standing on the small front stoop, Greg rang the doorbell and a dark-haired man dressed casually in faded jeans and a denim work shirt answered the door immediately. He slipped on a pair of wire-rimmed glasses, and then extended a hand to Greg in greeting.

"Lieutenant Garrison?"

"Yes. Thanks for inviting me here, Mr. Cutler."

"It's George. Please come in. I just made a fresh pot of coffee."

Greg followed him through an open foyer into the kitchen where the walls were lined with white cabinets, the counter tops were covered in white marble, and the floor was white ceramic tile. Must be hell to keep this room clean, Greg thought as he sat in the chair George held out for him and looked around the room.

George carried two cups of steaming coffee to the table where a pitcher of cream and a full sugar bowl had already been placed. "Please help yourself. You sounded surprised by what I told you on the phone. Ask your questions and I'll answer them as honestly as I can."

Greg nodded as he pulled a notepad from his breast pocket and turned to a blank page. "This case is a bit of a puzzle, to say the very least. Once I started doing some investigating, I discovered that the man who was murdered was not Joseph Armstrong. He was Philip Sharply. I haven't determined whether or not his wife's real name was Bette, but we'll get to that.

"Now, you sit here and tell me that Brenda Armstrong's name is really Tammy Cutler and she's your niece. On top of that, I find out her real father is David Cutler— your brother, and a new piece I have to fit into the puzzle.

"I guess my next question is, how long have you known this?"

George took a deep breath, exhaling slowly. "My mother passed away a year ago this past January. When I went through her papers, I found a large manila envelope addressed to her. The postmark date was May 1977. It was from a lawyer so I opened it."

Rising from his chair, George left the room for a moment and came back with what Greg assumed was the envelope, which he placed on the table, but didn't open.

"Turns out, it was from David's lawyer. There's a notarized statement from my brother inside, along with a hand-written letter to the lawyer instructing him to send everything to our mother should David die suddenly.

"David advised the lawyer not to share the contents of the envelope with the police because doing so would put Mom and me in grave danger. David though Mom should be the one to make that decision . . ."

Greg watched silently as the other man struggled to hold back tears. The anguish on his face was almost unbearable, but Greg knew the best thing to do was to give him some time. After a few moments, George managed to reign in his emotions, and with a loud snuffle, continued.

"There's also a family portrait in there—damn, this is really tough. It never gets any easier either. I was nine years old when David was killed."

"I'm sorry, George. I know it must be difficult to talk about all this—especially with a stranger, and I appreciate your candor." George nodded his thanks and Greg continued. "I don't understand how your brother's child became Brenda Armstrong."

"I'm getting to that. When David died in 1977, he had a two-year-old daughter— the girl you know as Brenda Armstrong, who was Tammy Cutler then. She's David's only child."

George paused, picked up both now empty cups, crossed the room to refill them, and then returned to his seat across from Greg, who was busily writing in his notepad. "Mom never knew what David was mixed up in. I'm sure she thought he really was a bookkeeper at the car dealership. Why she never did anything with the information he sent her is a mystery to me. I can only assume that she was afraid whoever killed David would come after me if she talked. So, she locked everything away in her trunk, which is where I found it."

"I didn't know there was a life insurance policy until after I read that information. My brother's death paid for my college education—I'm a Chemical Engineer. After I finished college, Mom took the remainder of the money and put a down payment on this house."

"But I still don't understand how your niece wound up with Sharply." Greg asked as he scribbled furiously in the notepad. There was too much information coming at him at one time and he knew if he didn't get it down on paper, he stood a chance of forgetting something important—something that might eventually shed some light on the ever-growing confusion behind the murders.

"Mom thought she would be raising Tammy after David's death and she was thrilled because, in a way, Tammy could keep David alive for her. You know, his child, carrying his blood in her veins—all of that stuff. And Mom loved Tammy. She thought the sun rose when that little girl walked into the room.

"Philip Sharply had other ideas, though. Both of the local papers covered the adoption proceedings and Mom clipped and saved every article about it. It's all there in the envelope with David's papers. She also cut out the articles relating to the car bomb that killed David and his wife, Carol.

"Sharply had the money and the lawyers to fight for custody of Tammy. The newspapers called him a prominent businessman who made his millions buying and selling used cars.

"He convinced the judge that not only was he more financially secure, but that he wanted custody of his best friend's child so that he could provide a safe and secure home for her. He promised the court that my mother could see her anytime she wanted to. And, he won."

George got up, paced the length of the room a few times, and then turned back to Greg.

"I took the family portrait of David, Carol and Tammy to a photo enhancement company that had the technology to digitally age Tammy so I'd have a good idea of what she would look like as an adult. When it was finished, I hired a private detective to try to locate her.

"We started with the assumption that she'd be in college somewhere so we began with the bigger schools on the east coast. The detective visited campuses and went through yearbooks, hoping for a break. He didn't find her so we began moving southward—it took a lot of time and a lot of money, but he finally found her this past January."

Greg listened, forgetting about his notes. "After locating her, did you make contact?"

George removed his glasses and rubbed his eyes. "Yes, I made my first phone call in January."

"Did she believe you?"

George closed his eyes for a second, shaking his head, and then put the glasses back on and stared at Greg. "No. Not at first. It took several calls to convince her."

"And how did you do that?"

"Like I said, it wasn't easy. I told her I had a picture of her taken with her parents when she was a child. She called me a liar— among other things. I asked her if she wanted to see it and she said yes. She gave me the address of a post office box where I could mail a copy of the photo. She called me about a week later, crying."

The two men stared silently at one another as George took a moment to gather his thoughts. "I asked her what was wrong and she told me she wanted to see the contents of the envelope. I told her I would send an airline ticket if she would fly up here to meet us. She said okay.

"She was here for two weeks—flew back home the evening before the murders. She promised to call, but she didn't. Then news about the murder was on the radio. Everyone was reporting that she had been hurt too."

Oh boy, Greg thought. How do I explain any of this to him when I don't even understand it myself? "Yes. We initially thought the younger woman at the house was your niece, but she claims to be someone else—Bethany Akin, Brenda's half-sister. What do you know about her?"

George stared at him, open-mouthed. "What? David only had one child— Tammy."

"Mr. Cutler—George, I don't know anything about your brother or Brenda

Armstrong. And I know very little about the girl in the hospital, but I do know she looks enough like Brenda to be her twin.

Shaking his head in denial, George turned away from him, but Greg pressed forward. "Let's assume for a moment that the young woman in the hospital is who she claims to be." He paused for a second before whispering, "So where is Brenda Armstrong?"

"I don't know," George said and the fear in his voice was genuine.

"Did she come back up here, George?"

"No! She flew back home just like I told you and I haven't seen her since."

Looking up at George, Greg nodded, convinced the man was telling the truth. "I'm not accusing you of anything, but if I don't ask, I'm not doing my job."

Shoulders slumped in exhaustion and suddenly feeling like a very old man, George crossed the room and sank back into his chair. "I shouldn't have let her leave."

There was no response Greg could offer that would make the other man feel better about the situation so he didn't try. "May I look inside the envelope?"

George looked from Greg to the envelope and back again "of course."

Turning envelope upside, Greg let contents slide out onto the table before removing the file from his briefcase that contained the FBI crime lab report along with photos of the Armstrong's and the information he'd gotten from Augusta.

The first newspaper clipping to catch his eye was about the twenty-year-old car bombing—including pictures of both victims David Cutler and his wife Carol. The images were faded and yellow, but Greg wasn't surprised to recognize the face of the woman he knew as Bette Armstrong staring up at him from the page.

Setting the clipping aside without comment, he skimmed through the articles about Sharply's adoption of the orphaned child of his best friend. This picture, too, was old and faded, but he could see that the man in the picture was the same as the one in the police photo from Augusta; the man known in Cleveland, Georgia as Joseph Armstrong.

The woman in the photo with Sharply who was identified as his fiancée was none other than the infamous Beatrice Langston––no surprise there either. There was a separate, smaller photo of Tammy Cutler, also known as Brenda Armstrong, who, according to the recent photo she'd left with her uncle when she'd visited, still looked very much the same.

Placing the clippings and his photos of the Armstrong's on the table in front of George, Greg pointed to the image of Sharply. "This is the man I know as Joseph Armstrong." Then he pointed at Carol, who had supposedly died with her husband in a car bombing twenty years earlier. "And this is the woman I know as Bette Armstrong. The woman identified here as his fiancée was his office manager in Cleveland—she's vanished into thin air.

"Tammy—I guess I should call her Brenda, told me the same thing when she looked at all of this stuff. If it's true, and I guess it must be, then who the hell was the woman who died in the car with David?"

Greg was silent for a moment before responding with an honest, "I have no idea."

George picked up the photo of Brenda. "She's the spitting image of my brother. It's almost like looking into his face. I hope what I'm thinking isn't true."

"What are you thinking?"

Ignoring the question for the moment, George laid the picture aside. "Do you have any leads on who killed them?"

Greg was slow to answer. He didn't want to offend this man with his suppositions, but he couldn't lie to him either. "George, I believe that Brenda Armstrong thought she had every reason in the world to kill her parents. Now that I've talked to you, my suspicions are stronger than ever."

George slammed his hand down on the table, staring wide-eyed at Greg. "You're wrong! There's no way she could be capable of murder, no matter what they did to her father."

"I can only imagine how hard this is for you to comprehend. But, you don't really know your niece that well."

"She's my brother's child, for God's sake!"

"And until recently, you haven't seen her since she was two and a half years old."

George shook his head in vehement denial. "She didn't do it."

"The Armstrong's had a safe deposit box, which contained, among other things, two life insurance policies—one for over a million dollars on Armstrong and the other for eight hundred thousand on his wife. Brenda is the beneficiary on both polices, which, in my opinion, gives her plenty of motive. Coupled with everything you've shared with me this morning, the case against her is just getting stronger and stronger.

"I know she's your niece and I know you love her, but if she is guilty of murder, it's my job to make sure she's arrested for it."

"She's my brother's only child," George whispered. "All I wanted was to get to know her and for her to get to know her real family. Other than that, I don't know anything at all." This time when the tears threatened, he didn't try to stop them. Instead, he let them roll unchecked down his cheeks where they collected in the lines at the corners of his mouth before he finally wiped them away with the back of a shaky hand.

"I am truly sorry, George."

The other man waved his condolences away impatiently. "Bawling like a baby," he said as he attempted to smile.

Greg smiled back before returning his

attention to the mass of papers on the tabletop, "would you mind if I made copies of all this?"

George gathered everything together and replaced it in the envelope. "Sure. I'll go with you. It's not that I don't trust you, it's just that this is all I have left of my brother and I don't plan to let any of it out of my sight."

"Do you know Philip Sharply's family?"

"I'd heard of Sharply before but didn't know him until I read all of this. But, I know his parents, Ruby and Clyde Sharply—law-abiding, God-fearing, fine people." George took the empty cups to the sink where he rinsed them before putting them into the dishwasher.

"After I read those papers I called Ruby just to talk, you know? I didn't want her to know what I'd discovered because Philip was their only son—three daughters, but only the one son. She brought up the subject of Philip on her own—seems he'd been on her mind a lot. According to her, he simply dropped off the face of the earth."

"What about your sister-in-law? How well do you know her people?"

George shrugged, "the Bentley's? They're just trying to make an honest living like most of the rest of us."

"Sure. I understand that." Greg placed his pen and notepad back in his shirt pocket. "I'd like to talk with Philip Sharply's parents. Could you help me?"

"I'll call them right now." George went to the telephone in the other room where Greg couldn't make out his words, only the low mumble of his voice as he spoke. Returning after a few moments, he told Greg that the Sharply's were anxious to speak with him.

Greg decided to do the visit before making copies of the envelope's contents and George agreed. When they arrived, Clyde Sharply opened the door before they'd had a chance to knock and ushered them in to the family room where Ruby waited, nervously chewing on an already ragged fingernail. As George made the introductions, Greg noticed how much Philip Sharply resembled his father.

Reluctant to tell these seemingly decent people what their son had been up to, Greg hemmed and hawed for a moment before Clyde asked him point blank to explain what was happening. "He may be our son, but we're not stupid people. We know he's been in trouble before."

"Your son has been using the name Joseph Armstrong for several years."

"You mean the Joseph Armstrong who was murdered down in Georgia?"

As Ruby gasped in surprise, Greg nodded. Clyde shook his head and gave a mirthless, little laugh.

"Something funny?" Greg asked.

Running a hand over his balding head, Clyde apologized for laughing. "Please don't think me insensitive or uncaring, detective. I don't really see any humor in this, but you have to understand that my boy's been dead to me for a long time—I already grieved for him.

"I think it's ironic that once he left here, Philip never contacted us, but, he still held on to the family."

Greg shook his head. "I'm sorry, but I don't understand."

"Joseph Armstrong—my father's first name was Joseph and my wife's maiden name was Armstrong. He didn't have much of an imagination, did he? We raised Philip to be a good boy, but things don't always work out the way we plan."

Crossing the room, he lifted a framed photo from its place on the mantle and carried it to Greg. "That's Philip when he was thirteen. I remember how he used to talk about being rich some day. He didn't seem to care what he had to do to make money as long as he made a lot of it."

The old man looked at the picture fondly

before speaking again—this time there was a slight tremor in his voice and Greg knew that no matter what he had said, Clyde still felt some pain in knowing his only son had been murdered. "I tried to tell him that kind of thinking would only lead to trouble, but he wouldn't listen."

Silent until now, Ruby loudly blew her nose on a whiter than white handkerchief and drew an audible breath before speaking. "I can't believe my son lived in Georgia all those years and never picked up the telephone to call me—not even on Mother's Day. I thought he must have died a long time ago, otherwise wouldn't a boy give his mother a call every now and again?" She sobbed loudly as she raised her hands to cover her eyes in an age-old gesture of grief and loss.

Clyde placed the picture back on the mantle, and then put his thin arms around his wife's heaving shoulders and patted her back tenderly. "Ruby, darlin' don't cry. You know I can't stand to see you cry."

Nodding, she lowered her hands and gave her husband a little smile before taking his hand and leading him to the sofa where they sat side by side, hands still clutched as they waited bravely for the next blow Greg might chose to deliver.

"Mr. and Mrs. Sharply, I am so sorry. Today seems to be my day for upsetting folks. But I have to do my job—even if it sometimes means upsetting people." They nodded their understanding and Greg continued with his questions. "How well do you know the Bentleys?"

Clyde and Ruby exchanged a glance before shaking their heads in unison. "We know Ernest and Jean in passing," Clyde explained. "But I wouldn't say we know them." Clyde said.

Greg stood. "Here's my card with my phone number. Do you think you could give it to them for me? I'm really pressed for time, but I'd like to talk with them."

"Be glad to," Clyde answered.

Greg clasped the old man's hand in his. "Sorry we had to meet under these circumstances. If either of you think of anything else, no matter how trivial it seems, please give me a call. You never know what might help."

Chapter Sixteen

On Wednesday morning, back in Georgia and ready to work, Greg arrived at the police station an hour earlier than his normal time, surprised to find Boswell already there and anxious to speak with him.

"I hope you found out something really good."

"You'll have to see it to believe it." Greg responded as he held up a large envelope from his briefcase. "I haven't read all of this yet, any volunteers to help?"

As he and Boswell headed for the conference room where they spread things out on the long table, Kate walked in. They motioned for her to join them.

"Okay," Boswell said. "Before we get started I want to know who the phone number belonged to and where you got all this information you're so eager to share."

Smiling, Greg slid a stack of papers out from under Boswell's hand and shook it at him. "The phone number belonged to George Cutler, who just happens to be Brenda Armstrong's uncle.

Brenda's real name is Tammy Cutler and her real father's name was David Cutler—he died in a car explosion about twenty years ago. My new friend George is David's brother. George found all of this stuff with his mother's belongings after she died."

"Are you serious?" Kate asked as Boswell smiled and said, "Good job, man."

Greg arranged the papers in neat stacks before passing some to Kate and some to the chief. "Yes ma'am, serious as a heart attack. But enough fun. We have a lot of reading to do." Pulling out a chair, he sat down and pulled another stack of papers to the edge of the table within arms reach, "any news from the hospital while I was gone?"

"Nope," Boswell answered.

"I want to visit Bethany Akin after we finish here."

"Why?" Kate asked, but Greg ignored her, choosing instead to start reading. Kate didn't push for an answer because she knew Greg would tell her what was on his mind when he was ready.

The first thing he picked up was the letter from David to his mother and Greg decided to skim it rather than read in detail. Cutler expressed love for his family, concern for his daughter, and fear for his own life, but there was nothing there that Greg hadn't heard from George yesterday. Laying the letter face down on the table, Greg picked up David's sworn statement, pulled out his notepad and pen so he could make notes, and began reading in earnest.

Cutler began by explaining that he had known Sharply since high school where he had started selling drugs at the age of fourteen—the market; after all, was huge, and then dropping out of school at seventeen because he needed to devote more time to his growing business. There were two other boys who had been involved right from the beginning, Bennie Trotter and Carl Manning, both of whom had dropped out of school along with Sharply—Cutler was the only one of the foursome to graduate.

Trotter became Cutler's commandeer-in chief, arranging pick-ups of their drug supply and stockpiling it in a warehouse rented by a dummy corporation. Manning supplied the drugs to other dealers and collected monies due up front. His dealers got reimbursed after they sold the drugs. Manning turned everything over to Trotter, who, in turn, passed all of the information along to Sharply.

In 1971, Sharply opened a used car dealership for the sole purpose to laundry the drug money that was deposited into the business account. Cutler was the bookkeeper and a woman named Janet Sigmore was the Certified Public Accountant. Between the two of them, they knew everything there was to know about laundering the drug money and making it come back clean and untraceable. They were so adept at their jobs that they even learned to produce dummy sales receipts for cars that were never sold, along with registrations, transfers of ownership and new tags—Massachusetts's sales taxes were carefully calculated for the "sold" vehicles and always submitted in a timely manner.

Unbeknownst to Sharply, Trotter was keeping some of the dealer's names, along with a small amount of money from each transaction, to himself in an attempt to build his own business. One of the dealers taped a conversation in which Trotter tried to convince him to drop Sharply and come in with him.

"Listen to this," Greg said. "Sharply originally had three partners—Cutler, a guy named Mike Trotter and another one named Carl Manning. According to Cutler, Manning was skimming a bit off the top of Sharply's drug business and got caught in the act.

"Sharply asked Trotter to meet him at their warehouse late one night, which apparently wasn't unusual—they met there on a fairly regular basis. Sharply confronted Trotter with the tape, but he denied everything—said it wasn't his voice and someone was trying to frame him.

"As far as Cutler knew, Sharply had never killed before, but he didn't have any qualms about doing it to protect his empire. Sharply knew Trotter carried a .45 in a shoulder holster and when he saw him reach for it, he pulled a 9mm Lugar, complete with silencer, from his pocket and blam—Trotter was dead from a single shot between the eyes before he hit the ground.

"At that point, Manning and Cutler, who had been watching from the shadows, stepped forward. Never losing his cool, Sharply ordered them to put Trotter's body into the trunk of his own car and drive it to a small lot located directly behind the Quincy police station. 'Wear gloves,' he ordered. Cutler knew Sharply had someone on the payroll at the Quincy PD but never found out his name." Greg tossed the statement onto the table.

"How could a man like Sharply live here for ten years without us ever knowing a thing about him?" Neither Kate nor Boswell had an answer for him, but Greg hadn't really expected one.

Kate raised her hand as if she were a student in class. "My turn," she said leaning forward in her chair. "Cutler married in 1972 and his wife gave birth to a daughter in '74. Carol Cutler knew what her husband did for a living, but it didn't matter to her because she liked the lifestyle that went along with the money.

"When Tammy—Brenda to us, was two years old, Cutler discovered that his wife and Sharply had been having an affair for several months. Cutler told her to stop and she refused. Desperate, Cutler threatened to go to the police and tell them what he did for a living and who he worked for if she didn't end the affair. She laughed in his face and told him he wouldn't dare because he'd be signing his own death warrant—he met with his attorney that afternoon."

"My turn," Boswell said as he held up a newspaper clipping. "Here's what happened to Manning. He got involved with a married woman, but when she discovered what he was, she broke it off. He didn't take kindly to the rejection and broke into her house one night, intending to kill her and the husband, who woke up and shot Manning six times with a little .22 he kept beside the bed for protection.

"No charges were ever brought against the husband—since Manning was dead on their bedroom floor with a gun in his hand, his intent was pretty obvious."

They sat in silence for a moment—Kate and Boswell lost in thought and Greg hoping one of them would pick up the article about the car bombing. He didn't have to wait long. Kate, who was idly sifting through the articles scattered across the table, suddenly snatched it up.

"Did you see this article?" she asked Greg. "It's dated two days after Cutler made his statement. Cutler and a woman presumed to be his wife were killed by a car bomb, leaving their two-year old daughter an orphan. The little girl was temporarily placed with her paternal grandmother." As she finished reading, Kate glanced at the accompanying photos. "Hey! This woman didn't die then. It's Bette Armstrong." Greg smiled and gave her an exaggerated wink. "I was hoping you'd notice that."

"Then who was the woman in the car with Cutler?" Boswell questioned.

Greg tossed the clipping about the adoption in front of them. "I have no idea. But, this story just keeps getting better. Read on."

Boswell and Kate leaned close to one another so they could read at the same time. When they finished reading, Boswell pushed the article aside, but Greg put it back in front of them again.

"According to George Cutler," he explained, "Soon after the adoption was finalized, Sharply his 'fiancée' and little Tammy disappeared—look at the woman in the picture more closely."

The pair studied the picture for a moment, and then Kate jumped to her feet as if she had received a jolt of electricity. "That's Beatrice Langston!"

"The lady gets first prize!"

Boswell raised a hand to massage his forehead. "I'm getting a headache. What's going on here?"

"What's bothering you, Boss?"

Boswell stood and began to pace the room as he talked. "Let's assume Sharply formed another drug ring right here in Cleveland. Who was his supplier and who sold the stuff? And, last, but not least, how did he get away with it right under our noses?"

He turned to face Greg. "One more thing—how is it that a woman who was killed in a car explosion could go unnoticed and live a happy-go-lucky life in our town?"

Greg shrugged. "The only answer I can come up with is that he had protection. Someone in our department must have been taking a payoff from Sharply."

Boswell shook his head in denial. "Don't you think I would know if one of my men was involved with something like that?"

Rising to his feet, Greg shouted back. "Don't yell at me. I wasn't the one. And what other explanation is there?"

Kate interrupted the shouting match to interject a thought of her own. "Maybe it's not at the local level," she said softly as she looked from one angry man to the other. "Maybe it's on the state level or higher."

"Higher?" Greg asked. "You mean on the federal level?"

"It wouldn't be the first time a federal agent turned dirty."

"Oh, God," Boswell groaned. "I don't even want to think about that." He picked up a stack of papers from the table, and then threw them back down in disgust. "All of this information is great but the question still remains—who murdered these two people?"

"That's easy," Greg responded, "the daughter."

Boswell slammed his hand down on the table. "Damn it, Greg. You've been trying to pin this on the daughter from day one."

"Yeah? And you think she's innocent? Then tell me where she is. Brenda Armstrong had motive."

"What about opportunity, Greg?" Kate asked. "And you seem to be forgetting about Beatrice Langston who conveniently transferred a huge amount of Armstrong's money into a brand new account, and then disappeared. What if way back when she really thought Sharply was planning to marry her only to realize at some point that he used her? It's possible that she waited a long, long time to get her revenge—stranger things have happened."

"Possible," Greg admitted. "But not probable. The money's another story though.

Okay, good points, Kate. Let's all calm down and review what we know up to this point. Brenda was two when her real father was killed— too young to remember him for very long. Sharply adopted her, changed his name, and reconnects with her real mother, who he married instead of Beatrice Langston.

"They left Massachusetts and changed their names. And they live a fairy-tale life for the next twenty years until Brenda's paternal grandmother dies and George Cutler finds the information we now have in front of us.

"George Cutler gambles that his niece is still alive somewhere and begins searching for her—finally finding her in Georgia and making contact. They meet and he gives her all of the information he gave me—she now has another motive."

Picking up David Cutler's sworn statement, he flips through a few pages until he finds the information he wants. "We also know the same type of gun that was used to kill Bennie Trotter was also used to kill the Armstrong's. According to Cutler, Sharply; therefore, Armstrong owned the original gun.

"I think he still owned it.

"Brenda Armstrong had plenty of opportunity. She came back into town the evening before the murders. What I don't know is if she confronted them with the information she had or if she just shot them as they enjoyed their morning coffee."

"Pretty good," Boswell said. "In theory anyway, so where are the gun and the knife?"

"Maybe still with her. Maybe she had

an accomplice who got rid of them for her. It's possible that Brenda and Beatrice Langston plotted the whole thing together—there was enough money for them to share and we know Langston went to the bank the morning of the murders."

Boswell snorted derisively. "And she could literally be anywhere in the world by now. Good as your story sounds, without the weapons and a corroborating witness, all of it's mere speculation on your part and not admissible in a court of law. In other words, you have didley squat."

"Well maybe it's time we had a talk with our mystery friend in the hospital. Maybe she knows something. I think I'll make a phone call to her doctor—Kate, you ready to go?" At her nod, he picked up the phone and began to dial.

Chapter Seventeen

Greg and Kate waited in the lounge for Dr. Hargrove, who seemed to be in no hurry to come find them. When at last he appeared, Greg introduced him to Kate, and then asked whether or not he thought Bethany Akin was up to talking with them.

Escorting them to his office before responding, Dr. Hargrove sat behind his desk and motioned for them to take seats as well. "I haven't pressed her, but I can ask her to join us."

As they waited, Dr. Hargrove moved the chair from the end of the couch to the side of his desk so it faced the detectives. At a knock, he crossed the room and opened the door.

"Beth, please sit here." He pointed, and then reseated himself. "This is Detective Greg Garrison, and his partner Sergeant Kate O'Connor. I explained to you that Detective Garrison was conducting the murder investigation."

Beth nodded at the two detectives. "I remember."

"Is it Beth or Bethany?" Greg questioned.

"Bethany is my full name," she explained. "But I like to be called Beth."

"Beth—not Brenda Armstrong?"

She nodded. "That's right."

Greg removed a small tape recorder from his pocket, placing it on the desk. "I want to record our conversation. I hope you don't mind."

She smiled and shook her head. "Of course not."

"Can you tell us what happened last Saturday?"

Her eyes widened in fear as she looked from one detective to the other. "I didn't murder anyone. You must believe me," she pleaded

"Beth, we're not here to accuse you. We simply need to know what happened."

Leaning forward, she whispered in

response, "They were already dead when I got there."

"Why don't you start at the beginning and tell us everything you remember. Try to relax—Dr. Hargrove will be here the whole time."

Nodding, she drew a deep breath and began. "I got up before daybreak on Saturday, drank a few too many cups of coffee to bolster my courage, and then left for the Armstrong's house.

"There's an empty lot a bit past their house the driveway's in, but . . . I don't know anything about building houses. I guess someone was planning to build but there's nothing else there. I pulled in there to keep my car in the shade of the trees and walked back towards their house. I didn't think I'd be long so I left my handbag and the keys tucked under the front seat." She shrugged in Kate's direction as if she thought another woman might understand more than a man would. "I just hate carrying those things all the time.

"It must have been around seven by then—I don't wear a watch so I'm not exactly sure. It was early enough that there were no lights on in any of the other houses yet, at least not that I could see. I was nervous shaking so badly I could barely walk straight. I almost turned around and left, but I'd come so far and I had to confront the people who had killed my parents."

Greg and Dr. Hargrove jumped to their feet at the same time. "Killed your parents?" Greg asked.

Beth looked from one man to the other. "Please let me finish before you ask me any questions. Please?"

Ignoring her request, Dr. Hargrove stared at her. "Beth, when you first came in here, you thought you'd just given birth to a baby girl. When I asked you about your parents, you told me they had come into the hospital and taken the baby—you were sure they planned to kill her. Upon further questioning, you claimed they died in a car accident many years ago. Are you sure that's how they died?"

"Yes. Now please let me finish my story." Dr. Hargrove nodded at Greg and both men reseated themselves as she continued.

Satisfied they would listen, Beth picked up the thread of her story. "I walked to the door and rang the door bell. I thought I heard someone walking around inside—it sounded like they were coming to the door, but they didn't. So I rang the doorbell again, still no answer. I banged the brass knocker against the door and it opened slightly."

She crossed her arms, hugging herself as if seeking comfort from the horror she'd witnessed. "I pushed it open a bit further and stuck my head in, calling out 'Hello,' but no one answered. I stepped into the foyer the living room to the left was dark, but I sensed that someone was there so I called out again"

Tears coursed down Beth's pale face as she stood and crossed the room to the window. Greg moved as if to get up and follow her, but Kate's hand on his arm and a stern look from Dr. Hargrove stopped him.

"That's when I looked across the room into the kitchen. I saw the blood before I saw the man sprawled on the floor. I must have gone into shock because I know I was moving toward him, not the other way around, but it felt as if the floor were rolling or something and instead of me moving, he was coming closer and closer and I had no control. I remember thinking someone was playing a cruel joke on me.

"As soon as I reached the kitchen doorway, I saw the woman on the floor she was leaning against the cabinet under the oven. I looked away, looked down my feet and saw that I was standing in blood. I wanted to scream opened my mouth to do it but nothing would come out.

"I didn't want to look at their faces but I

couldn't help it. Both of them seemed to be staring back at me with accusatory eyes like the whole thing was somehow my fault, but it wasn't.

"The realization of what had happened finally hit me and I turned to run, to get out of there as fast as I could. That's when I felt a sharp pain in my back that knocked me to the floor. I think I hit my head when I fell and it knocked me out.

"When I woke up, I was lying next to the dead couple, right in the middle of all that blood. I tried to get to my feet several times but they kept slipping in the blood. Every time I managed to struggle upward a bit, the excruciating pain in my back would knock me down again. I don't know how many times I tried, but when I finally managed to stand, I found myself looking into his eyes again. I couldn't take any more it was painful to move, but I ran, or tried to, as fast as I could to get out of that house and into the fresh air."

Beth closed her eyes and her slight frame shook as a flood of tears streamed down her face. Greg turned to Kate and saw her wiping at tears of sympathy with the back of her hand. When he turned back around, Dr. Hargrove had crossed the room to escort Beth back to her chair. He murmured words of comfort to her, and then handed her a tissue.

"Do you need a break?" Greg asked.

Beth wiped her face and shook her head. "I'm okay."

"Beth, there is no doubt in my mind that you are Brenda Armstrong's half-sister. I've never met her, but I've seen a picture and you two could pass for twins. But I'd like to know which parent you have in common?"

"We have the same father."

"Your father is David Cutler?"

"Yes."

He leaned back needing a moment to absorb this new bit of information. "Do you know where Brenda is?"

"No, and I've been here since the middle of March looking for her."

Greg looked at Kate, who seemed to be so saddened by Beth's story. A rush of tenderness for her overwhelmed him he wanted to take her into his arms and comfort her. Comfort Kate rather than Beth who had lived through the ordeal. Forcing him self to look away before he made a complete and utter fool of himself by picking her up and rocking her in his arms, he asked another question.

"How often do you and Brenda get together?"

"I've never met my sister, Detective."

"Then how did you know where she lived?"

"Detective, please let her tell us in her own words. Beth, go ahead—start from the beginning."

"I didn't know anything about my parents until January of this year when Aunt Bee came to see me at the University of Virginia where I go to college. She told me my mom's name was Suzanne Akin and my dad's name was David Cutler—they had never married. That's when I found out I had a sister. I was so excited to find out that I actually had a family."

"Wait a minute. Aunt Bee?"

Beth nodded. "Her name is Beatrice Langston but I've always called her Aunt Bee."

Greg turned to Kate, who had snapped to attention, all traces of sadness gone from her face, at the mention of Beatrice Langston.

Greg turned back to Beth. "I'm sorry. Go on."

Beth blew her nose. "I wanted to meet my sister right then. But Aunt Bee told me that Brenda didn't know about me."

"I asked her and she told me Brenda didn't know about her <u>real</u> father so she couldn't tell her about me. That's when she gave me three diaries that had belonged to my mother.

"All my life, I've wanted to know something about my parents. I knew Aunt Bee knew who they were but she wouldn't talk about them. That day, she told me about my father and what he was involved in before he died. She also told me about my mom and dad getting killed when I was two and a half years old.

"The woman I'd always known as Aunt Bee was really a friend of my mother's who put me in an orphanage after Mom was killed."

Kate crossed the room to stand next to Beth. "If your Aunt Bee loved you so much, why didn't she keep you?" she questioned.

Beth twisted the tissue between her hands. "When Brenda's mom found out about me, she was furious she wanted me dead." Beth looked out into the distance. "Aunt Bee knew she'd have to hide me to keep me safe. She and my mom were raised in Mother Mary's Orphanage outside of Roanoke, Virginia and that's where I was raised too."

"I couldn't believe my luck everything I could possibly want to know about my mother was in those diaries. The first one started when she was ten and ended when she was thirteen. The next one ended when she was twenty and the last one ended the day she died."

She turned to Kate, her eyes brimming with righteous anger. "I was so angry with Aunt Bee that day. Not only did she have the diaries but she also had pictures dating all the way back to the day my mother started school and continuing until a few days before she died. There were even pictures of me with my mother and several pictures of Mom and Dad together."

Greg leaned forward in his chair. "But they were killed in Quincy, Massachusetts not Virginia. David Cutler was married and had a child. Were your parents having an affair?"

Beth nodded. "After college, Mom and Aunt Bee moved to Massachusetts where my parents met." She paused to blow her nose. "According to Mom's diary, she knew Dad was engaged when she started seeing him. And she knew he wasn't going to break it off to be with her. She didn't care because she loved him so much.

"The affair lasted almost a year. Mom didn't know she was pregnant until after it ended. To my mom, having a family was a gift from God being pregnant by the man she loved was the best thing that could have happened to her.

"When I was almost two and a half, Mom came down with ovarian cancer. The doctors said she only a few months to live. She was terrified that I would end up being raised the way she was so she called my father to ask him to meet her to discuss something important."

She began to cry again. "She made the last entry in her diary a few hours before she left to meet him. Aunt Bee said the car exploded a few blocks from our house Mom was bringing him to meet me."

No one spoke for a minute as they tried to digest everything that Beth had told them. "You know," she said at last. "I've called her Aunt Bee all my life, but that's not her real name."

"What is her real name?" Greg asked with genuine interest. This one little clue might help to tie everything together.

"Janet Sigmore," she replied.

"When did you start trying to find Brenda?" interjected Kate.

"When Aunt Bee told me about Brenda she said she was a student at the University of Georgia. So I left college during the second week of March and came down here. I requested a copy of Brenda's class schedule at the administration office I think the woman thought I was her and she was too lazy to ask for identification. I didn't tell her differently. I went to the class where she should have been but she never showed up. She wasn't in any of her other classes either. I followed her schedule for several days and she never showed up.

"One day I was in the library and this girl handed me a folded note from someone at the BETA house again, someone thought I was her and again I didn't tell her any differently. The note stated that when Brenda moved from the sorority house she'd left behind some things. That's how I found out she no longer lived on campus. I found her apartment on College Avenue but she wasn't there either.

Dr. Hargrove, who'd been fairly silent throughout the session, spoke up. "Beth, how did you find out where the Armstrong's lived?"

She smiled at him, "Another stroke of good luck and mistaken identity. I had returned to the administration building to see if I could find out anything else about Brenda and a woman approached me I think Brenda must have worked there part time because the woman seemed to know her. She explained that the letter came to their office because it had been addressed wrong. When she saw it, she held on to it because she knew she'd be seeing me, meaning Brenda, of course, soon.

It was from Brenda's mother who obviously hadn't been told her daughter moved because she was still writing to her at the BETA house. There was a return address on the envelope and that's how I knew where to look next."

"So you came to Cleveland in mid-March and never left?" Greg asked.

"Yes. I rented one of the cabins up at Turners Corner, just the other side of Cleveland. It's in under my name."

"Those cabins are expensive, Beth" Kate pointed out. "How did you pay for it?"

"Mom had a accidental death insurance at work a double indemnity policy. The money was put into a trust fund for me and I started receiving payments when I turned eighteen"

Kate, who had believed Beth up until this point became suspicious. "According to old newspaper accounts, it was Carol Cutler who died in the car with her husband. In order for your mother's insurance to pay off, there had to be a death certificate. Something's not right here."

Beth shrugged. "I don't have the answers to that. All I know is what Aunt Bee told me."

In addition to using the tape recorder, Greg was also taking notes and he flipped back through them before turning to Beth again. "You said you left college in March to come down here. How did you get here? Did you fly or drive? Do you own a car or did you rent one?"

She nodded, "Yes, I have a car, but I didn't drive here. I flew from Norfolk, and then rented a car at the Atlanta Airport, which is also in my name."

Greg stared at her for a moment. "You said you left your purse and keys inside the car?"

"That's right. And in the trunk, you'll find a box with my mother's diaries inside." Detective Garrison, you've got to believe me. I didn't kill anyone."

"I believe you, Beth. And I want to help you, but you need to be very careful for awhile. I don't want you to leave this hospital unless it's with Sergeant O'Connor or me. Do you understand?" Wide-eyed, she nodded. Greg turned to Dr. Hargrove. "You won't let her leave, will you?"

Dr. Hargrove stood. "Detective, when she feels she's ready to leave, I can't make her stay though I can recommend that she remain for a bit longer if that will help."

Greg nodded. "Thanks.

"I won't leave without one of you," Beth promised

Greg stood, turned off the tape recorder and returned it to his pocket. "I want to have your car towed to our garage and have the Georgia Bureau of Investigation's crime lab look it over. It's possible that whoever killed the Armstrong's found your car and left fingerprints on it."

"Detective, do you know where my Aunt Bee is?"

Greg shook his head. "She came to see me the night of the murders, but we haven't been able to locate her since then."

"I said some dreadful things to her I hope nothing bad has happened."

"I'm sorry Beth, but I can't honestly offer you any reassurance. I don't know where she is. But if it's any comfort, and it's probably not, her body hasn't been found.

"Thanks for your time, Beth. Dr. Armstrong. We'll be in touch."

Chapter Eighteen

The day threatened to be another scorcher and the humidity was already so high that by the time they reached the car, Greg and Kate were both damp with sweat. Greg started the car and turned on the air conditioner, releasing a refreshing blast of cool air into their faces. Finally turning to Kate, he asked if she was all right.

Shaking her head, Kate avoided his gaze. "I guess I'm just a softie. Any time someone else is sad or cries, I can't help but cry too."

Hesitant but determined, Greg put the car in gear and pulled slowly out of the parking lot. "Kate, do you think would you go out with me sometime?"

"Greg Garrison you sly devil! I didn't think you'd even noticed me. Yes, I'd love to go out with you."

Now that he'd asked and she'd answered, Greg felt his confidence return. Slipping on his sunglasses, he smiled. "What about tonight? Come over to my house and I'll throw a couple of steaks on the grill."

"That sounds like fun. What time?"

"Why don't you just follow me home from work?"

"No. I want to go home and change first. Give me directions you can write them down when we get back to the office."

He nodded his agreement. "Where do you think Brenda Armstrong is hiding?"

"I have no idea, but she must know what happened to her parents. It's been all over the television and newspapers for days. I keep thinking she'll show up at any minute."

Greg didn't respond and Kate turned to watch him as he easily maneuvered the car through heavy traffic. "You know," she said with a hint of a smile. "You are kind of cute."

"Yeah, so are you."

They both laughed as if the brief exchange had been one of the funniest things they'd ever heard then fell into a comfortable silence. As they neared the crime scene, Greg felt the muscles in his stomach tighten, his breathing become more rapid and his heart rate accelerate. As if sensing his unease, Kate offered him a reassuring smile it worked.

He took a deep breath as he glanced at the house surrounded by yellow crime scene tape and eased his foot off of the accelerator. If Beth was telling the truth, her car should be somewhere right up ahead. They spotted it at the same time a glint of silver sunlight off the rear bumper. Kate pointed and he nodded as he turned into the driveway behind the dark blue Chevy Caprice, put his car in park and cut the ignition.

Greg walked slightly ahead of Kate, both of them half-expecting to see a body or at the very least blood in or around the car. They were not disappointed; however, when they peered through the rain-splattered windows to see nothing of the sort. Removing a handkerchief from his jacket pocket, Greg used it to test the door handle, which opened easily to release a cloud of musty, stale air and nothing else.

With an audible sigh of relief, he turned to Kate. "I'll call the Chief."

As they waited for the forensics team to show up with a tow truck, Kate leaned against Greg's car and looked up at him with wide eyes. Confused by the fear he saw there, Greg stared down at her. "What's wrong, Kate? You're not afraid of me, are you?"

"I'm not very comfortable with men," she confessed.

"What? Why?"

Laughing nervously, she shook her head and avoided his gaze. "Let's not talk about it, okay?"

Putting a finger under her chin and tilted her face up so he could look into her eyes. "I would never hurt you, Kate."

Although his touch had been gentle, she

jerked as if she'd been slapped. "Please don't crowd me."

What is wrong, he thought as he stepped back a pace to give her the space she needed. "Hey," he said softly. "I'm the same guy you've been working with every day. How can you be afraid of me now?"

"I it's different when we're working. I can't explain it. Listen, Greg. Maybe my coming to your house this evening is not such a good idea."

"Tell me what I've done."

"It's not you. It's me."

"Are you afraid of all men or just me?" She pushed herself away from the car and turned to walk away, but he placed a restraining hand on her arm she stopped but didn't look at him. "Talk to me, Kate."

"I don't date. I've never dated. I've tried to I've even gone as far as making a date, but end up canceling at the last minute. It's not you, it's me," she repeated.

"What's the problem?"

She pulled her arm from his grasp and shook her head. "I don't want to talk about it. I can't talk about it."

The sound of an approaching car caught his attention and he turned just as Chief Boswell pulled his car into the driveway and parked. He turned to Kate, desperate to resolve things before work and other people caused further distraction. "Please come to my house tonight. I won't touch you, but I do want to spend some time with you."

Ignoring his plea, Kate turned to watch the approach of Chief Boswell, who began asking questions before he'd emerged all the way from his vehicle. "Does that car belong to the girl in the hospital?"

Sighing at the missed opportunity to connect with Kate, Greg stepped into the role of detective instead of prospective date and nodded. "Yes. She rented it at the airport. Did you call GBI.?"

Sensing something amiss between the two detectives, Boswell looked from one to the other before giving Greg a questioning look. "What's wrong? You sound like you've lost your best friend?"

Grateful for the appearance of the tow truck at the end of the driveway, Greg changed the subject. "The truck's here. We need to move our cars."

Boswell looked at Kate. "What's eating him?" She shrugged and stepped out of the way so Greg could move the car as soon as Boswell moved his.

Silent as they drove back to the station, Kate turned to Greg as they pulled into the parking lot. "I want to come to your house tonight because I want to spend time with you too. But, Greg, you've got to give me room. Please understand."

Removing his sunglasses, he stared into her eyes for a moment before nodding. "Okay. We'll do it your way, sometime around seven?"

"I'll be there."

Back at his desk, Greg thumbed through the information from George Cutler, stopping to remove the report about Benny Trotter's murder there was nothing relative in it. Finding the report about the car explosion that killed David Cutler and Suzanne Akin, which was what he wanted, he settled in to do some serious reading. He laid the police photos side by side on his desk and shook his head in amazement as he began to read the investigating officer had determined the explosion was caused by mechanical failure.

He looked closer at the photos mechanical explosion? That couldn't be right. The photos clearly showed that the hood of the vehicle had been sheared off at the windshield, not from underneath, which would indicate an explosion in the engine itself. The driver's seat had been blown backwards off its mount and the passenger seat had torn its way through the right door. The top of the car an almost unrecognizable mass of crumpled metal lay on the ground several feet behind the remains of the car. What was left of the interior was charred it made his stomach churn to think about what the bodies must have looked like when they were peeled from the wreckage. No way was this destruction caused by mechanical failure. It was evident that the findings of the police report were flawed.

Searching for the name of the investigating officer, Greg felt a tingle of apprehension when he found it Lieutenant Carl Goodwin, the same detective who'd investigated the murder of Benny Trotter. Could there a connection between Trotter, Cutler and Goodwin? Trotter and Cutler had both worked for Philip Sharply, aka Joseph Armstrong. Was George Cutler right? Had Sharply murdered David Cutler? And was Goodwin involved a crooked cop? Any arrest would have to come from the police report filed by the detective, but since he determined the cause of explosion was due to a mechanical failure, no arrests were ever made and the file had been closed.

Unanswered questions tumbled over one another in Greg's head and he began to write them down so as not to lose track of anything. How had George Cutler gotten copies of the police report in the first place? Was Goodwin covering up for Sharply and did he still work for the Quincy Police Department? Did George Cutler go to the Quincy Police Station to find out more about his brother's death and meet Goodwin? Is that how they tracked down Armstrong? Too many questions, he thought, and no resources available right now to answer any of them. He called George Cutler's home and was disappointed when the answering machine picked up. Leaving his name and home number, he asked George to call him as soon as he got in.

I'm _so_ tired, he thought. I need some air and some exercise. Scribbling directions for Kate on a blank sheet of paper, he left them in her chair so she'd be sure to find them when she came back from wherever she'd disappeared to. Boswell was out too, so he left him a voice mail telling him that he was taking off early if he didn't breathe some clean air for awhile, he'd be no good to anyone.

As soon as he entered his house, Greg changed into running clothes, clipped a Walkman to his waistband, placed the headphones over his ears and left the house. Jogging out of the driveway he turned left on Walter O'Malley Road moving away from the busy highway and towards the not-so-distant mountains. His pace increase with the tempo of the country music he listened to, but try as he might, he couldn't think of anything other than the case. More unanswered questions moved as quickly through his head as his feet did on the pavement.

Why hadn't the car explosion been questioned more closely by anyone? Was the gun used to kill Benny Trotter the same one that had been used to commit the gruesome murders here? Had Sharply kept it, brought it with him, only to have it turned against him by some, as yet, unknown assailant? And where were Brenda Armstrong and Beatrice Langston? His gut tightened as if in protest against all the questions, but he couldn't stop them. He wondered if the murderer was still in Cleveland and if it could be the mysterious stranger who had accompanied Beatrice Langston to the bank on the day of the murders.

Reaching his set turn around point some four miles from the house, he turned, jogging in place for several moments, and then began the return run. Soaked with perspiration as he ran into his own backyard, he removed the headphones and walked around a bit to bring his heart rate back to normal and allow himself the chance to cool off. As he walked at the far edges of the yard, he thought he heard a phone ringing?

Is that my phone, he thought as he dashed toward the house? Yes fumbling for the key he'd dropped into the small pocket of his shorts as he'd left, he finally managed to let himself in and raced across the room to pick up a phone he was sure would quit ringing the second he did.

"Hello?"

"Detective Garrison," The woman on the other end asked

"Yes?"

"Do you remember talking to me?"

"I don't know. Who are you?" Turning to the sink, he filled a tumbler with cold water and held it to his forehead for a moment before taking a long, refreshing drink.

"Beatrice Langston. Now, do you remember me?"

"Yes, of course. Where are you?"

"I can't tell you that. Not yet anyway. How's Beth?"

"Beth is fine. She's safe."

"Has she met Brenda yet?"

"Miss Langston, no one can find Brenda Armstrong. Why don't you tell me what you know about all of this? And don't try to tell me you don't know anything because I know better."

There was a slight pause on the other end. "Yes, I know a lot and I have proof. The information I have dates all the way back to the early seventies."

"Then come back here and bring your proof with you."

"If I did that, Lieutenant, I'd have a life expectancy of about five minutes."

"I'd protect you."

"You would? You can't protect your own department from the dirty cop who's working there. How do you think you can protect me from that very same person?"

Deciding to trust her, at least for the moment, Greg responded. "I had a feeling someone on the inside was involved how else could Armstrong run his operation for so long without being detected? If you know who it is then tell me."

"I can't do that."

"In other words, you don't know."

She laughed. "Don't try that game with me, Lieutenant. I am not a child who will respond with 'Oh yes, I do. It's so and so.' I am planning to keep myself alive for as long as I can and I cannot do that by telling you who the dirty cop is."

"So why did you call?"

"Have you been to Quincy?" Nodding as if she could see him, Greg responded affirmatively.

"I'm assuming David's brother told you how he died?"

"Yes. He also provided me with a police report about the 'accident'."

"Do you believe the report?"

"I find it very hard to believe that it was an explosion caused by mechanical failure."

"Good for you. I know it was a car bomb, and I know who made the bomb and put it in David's car. Did you see the investigating officer's name?"

"Carl Goodwin. Was he dirty?"

She laughed. "What do you mean was? He still is. Detective, I think you're an honest person who will do the right thing. I'll make a deal with you you go back to Quincy and set the record straight for David and my sweet Beth because that child never hurt anyone. Then you'll know who your dirty cop is. When that filthy, no-good cop is arrested, I'll turn everything I have over to you. But only to you."

"I don't know if there's anything I can do in Quincy, especially after so many years, but I'll give it my best shot."

"I'd also like to suggest, Lieutenant, that you not discuss my phone call with anyone other than Chief Boswell. Believe me when I tell you, if you do, you will blow this case apart. Do we have a deal?"

"For now, when will I hear from you again?" The only response was a click and

the buzzing of the dial tone in his ear shit!
She'd hung up. He crossed the room to look
at the caller ID unknown name. No help
from that quarter either.

Already stripping off his clothing as he
strode through the house to the bathroom,
Greg turned on the cold water in the shower
and stood under the refreshing spray for
several moments before washing the sweat
and grime of a long day from his skin. Then,
dried and dressed, he went outside to start
the grill. As he came back in and opened the
refrigerator to remove the steaks, the
doorbell rang.

Chapter Nineteen

Kate changed into white shorts and a light pink cotton top and her black hair glistened as a ray of fast-fading sunlight danced behind her head. Her dark eyes reminded him of bright new marbles—not very romantic, but that's what they made him think of. "Wow, look at you!" he exclaimed, ushering her into the house.

She followed him into the kitchen. "Anything you want me to do?"

He winked at her and then smiled to show he was teasing. "Just stand there and look pretty."

"You seem mighty happy."

He stopped in the middle of pulling salad fixings from the refrigerator to stare at her seriously. "Why shouldn't I be happy? I'm spending the evening with the prettiest woman in Georgia." He paused for a second, and then with a what-the-hell shrug of his broad shoulders, continued. "Who, I might add for those who might be interested, I'm crazy about. Life is good."

Kate watched as he began to tear the lettuce into bite-sized pieces. "Greg, you don't know anything about me."

"That's why I want to spend some time with you. I want to get to know you."

"We spend all day together."

"I know. And when the day's over, I don't want to let you go."

"You may not like me once you get to know me," she whispered.

The ringing of the telephone cut off his response. "Excuse me, Kate. I really need to answer that. Hello? Hi, Chief."

"I hope you haven't made any plans for the evening."

"As a matter-of-fact, I did. Why? What's wrong?"

"I just got a call from Athens PD they found the body of a young woman on the university campus about an hour ago."

Greg felt a sense of dread as he asked the next question. "Why'd they call you?"

"A professor identified the young woman as Brenda Armstrong."

"I knew it," Greg said, raising a hand to his massage his suddenly aching temples. "What happened?"

"One shot to the back of the head and one through the back they think it entered her heart."

Kate crossed the room to stand at his side and he gratefully reached out to grasp the hand she offered. "We need to get over there."

"Good idea. Do you want to call Kate or should I?"

"Don't bother. She's standing right here."

People outside of law enforcement might not understand how Boswell could joke at a time like this, but police officers knew that it was essential for their sanity to be able to find humor wherever and whenever possible. "You sly dog," he teased now. "Do I detect a hint of romance in the air? Young love in bloom and all that mush?"

"Mush?" Not with Kate, he thought. "I don't think so the rest, we'll see. I'll let you know what we find in Athens." He hung up and turned to Kate. "Looks like our dinner plans are on hold for now."

"What's happening?"

"Brenda Armstrong turned up dead shot twice."

"Dear Lord where?"

Greg put his arms around her to pull her close for a moment. "Athens. On the UGA campus,"

He felt Kate tense as she pulled away from his embrace with a shake of her head. "Please don't."

Unsure of what to do, he took a step toward her, and then stopped. He wanted to hold her yet he didn't want to frighten her. "Talk to me Kate. What are you so afraid of? What happened to you?"

"I already told you that I don't want to talk about it it's not you, Greg."

"Then who was it?"

"Enough," Kate said and he heard the anger in her voice. "I'm going home to change. Do you want to pick me up or should I meet you there?"

"I'll pick you up. Please talk to me, Kate. Don't shut me out."

"Do you know where I live?"

"Yeah, I know."

"Don't forget to turn off the grill. I'll wait for you outside my apartment." She left, slamming the door behind her.

From the bay window in the den, Greg watched Kate get into her car, back out of his driveway and speed away. He turned the grill off, and then wrapped the food and put it back into the refrigerator. He changed his clothes and went to pick up Kate, who, as promised, was waiting for him outside her apartment. She got in and fastened her seatbelt.

"I don't suppose you want to talk."

Laying her pure on the floorboard, she shook her head. "No. It's my personal hell and I'll deal with it. Thanks anyway."

Lost in their own thoughts, neither detective spoke as they made the drive to Athens. There was a large crowd gathered in one of the campus parking lots and Greg guessed correctly that they were near the crime scene. Showing his badge to the chubby officer who had been assigned to crowd control allowed him to maneuver through the mass of bodies and park along the curb behind two patrol cars and an ambulance all of them empty but with lights flashing, which was what had drawn many of the curious here in the first place.

As they exited the vehicle, both Greg and Kate automatically pulled their badges out of pockets and clipped them to their belts where they would be visible to the other detectives and uniformed officers working the crime scene. There was no need to ask for directions to the crime scene, they simply followed the crowd past a three-story, red brick building and down a dirt path that lead into the woods. As they neared the yellow crime tape already in place the crowd thinned and a uniformed officer stepped forward to meet them, "Detectives Garrison and O'Connor from Cleveland?" Greg nodded. "We've been expecting you."

For a moment Greg felt an urge to laugh at the oddly formal statement as if they'd arrived late to a party or something. But when he glanced at Kate and saw how pale her face had gone the urge dissipated as quickly as it had come.

"Go on through the tape, detectives. Lieutenant Leroy Allen is in charge. You can't miss him he's about six-five, hair in cornrows and the only black guy in there."

"Thanks," said Greg, stepping forward to lift the tape and follow Kate down the path.

Allen looked up as they approached. "There you are," he greeted them in a voice that was much softer than one might expect from such a big man. "I'm Leroy Allen, the poor fool who's in charge of this mess." He held up his gloved hands for their inspection. "Excuse me for not offering to shake hands, but as you can see—"

They nodded their understanding. "Greg Garrison and this is my partner Kate O'Connor. Chief Boswell said the girl was positively identified as Brenda Armstrong."

"That's right. One of her professors did the ID."

Greg looked past the detective to the white-sheeted body. "She was shot?" he asked.

"Let me show you," he said as he turned to lead them the few feet to the victim and bent to flip back the sheet. Leroy pulled a flashlight from a loop on his belt and shone it on the body, which was lying face down.

"Her hands are tied behind her with a

short length of rope and there's what appears to be a silk scarf covering her mouth." He moved the beam of the flashlight to show them the entry wounds. "One bullet through the back of the head and another one through the back probably entered her heart."

He replaced the sheet, and then stood up again. "I can't be one hundred percent certain that the second bullet penetrated the heart until the autopsy is completed. But, if I was a gambling man, and I am, I'd say it's a pretty sure thing."

"This path seems pretty well-worn lots of traffic passing back and forth. Where does it lead?" Greg asked.

Ducking under a low-hanging branch, Leroy moved forward, motioning for them to follow. "I'll show you." He stopped at a narrower path, which was almost hidden from view by the dense foliage. "College officials discourage students from using paths like this, especially late in the evening or early in the morning."

Leroy led them through the underbrush, which slapped at their faces and exposed skin with every step. He finally stopped at the edge of a fairly large clearing. "This is used mostly by first-year students who are away from home for the first time. Mom and Dad aren't around to tell them no and some of these kids seem to think they have to prove how grown-up they are.

"They want a little hanky panky once in a while and this is a popular spot for it." He shone his flashlight around the perimeter of the clearing to show them the cover offered by the trees and brush, "very secluded."

When neither Greg nor Kate said anything, he turned and led them back down the path and out of the underbrush and stood facing the body. "Around six this evening, a young Romeo came here with his girlfriend. They entered the underbrush from the street end through a hole in the fence. They got to right here and discovered the body, which, I imagine, put a real damper on their romantic mood."

He led them down to the fence. "That's Hull Street. As you can see, the body is partially visible even from here."

"Do you have an idea as to when she was killed?" Greg asked.

Leroy flipped open his note pad. "I talked to three sophomores, Deborah McDougal, Peggy Stanley, and Barbara Norton, who live together in a boarding house on Huff Street. According to their statements, they left the library around four-thirty and came through here the body wasn't here then."

He flipped several pages. "Chad Holcombe and Tara Harrison are the couple who found the body. Like I said, they came through around six and there she was." He shrugged as he flipped the note pad closed and turned to Greg. "It's a no-brainer. The murder took place between four-thirty and six o'clock. The coroner may be able to narrow it down a little, but that's pretty tight."

"Any idea what caliber of gun was used?" Greg asked.

"The shot to the head went clean through, but we haven't found the bullet yet. The other one is still in there so we'll know more once it's been removed."

"Tell me about the professor who identified her"

"When Chad Holcombe saw the body, he ran to get help and the first person he saw was Professor Helton." He pointed up the hill to a woman standing beside a picnic table. "That's her if you want to talk to her."

"Thank you. I think we will." Greg turned to Kate and asked her softly if she was okay no sense in drawing anyone else's attention to the fact that she was paler than pale and covered in sweat.

"Yeah I'm fine."

"You do get used to it after awhile. I don't know if that's a good thing or not, but it helps get you through." He turned in the direction of Professor Helton, "you coming?"

"You go ahead. I think I'll hang around here for a bit." She turned to Leroy. "That is, if you don't mind."

"Not at all, detective," he responded with smile.

Chapter Twenty

She stood at the far end of the picnic table, arms crossed under her breasts, watching his approach through calm blue eyes. The nearby lights from the parking lot illuminated her pale blonde hair, a few stray tendrils drifted across her face, but she didn't bother to brush them away, seemed almost unaware of their presence. Greg lowered his head for a moment to hide a smile this woman knew what she looked like, knew the lighting was the perfect backdrop for her pale beauty and was taking full advantage of it even as she waited to be questioned about identifying the body of one of her students.

"My name is Detective Greg Garrison. I'm with the Cleveland Police Department up in White County." He motioned to one of the table's attached benches. "Can we sit down for a few minutes?"

"Detective Allen said you might want to speak with me." She sat, turning the full force of her gaze upon him, but Greg didn't notice. As he sat across from the woman, he realized he had the perfect view of Kate who still stood with Leroy Allen at the bottom of the hill. He watched her for a moment as he retrieved the ever-present notepad and pen from his pocket, and then turned his attention back to the task at hand.

"Detective Allen said you identified the body."

"Yes, Brenda was one of my students."

"Are you positive that it's her?"

"Of course, it's Brenda."

Greg turned his head to stare into the blue eyes that were watching him with a bit too much interest. The professor was a very attractive woman, but it was Kate who'd already captured his heart. She shifted her position slightly so that her leg was mere inches away from his under the table what an attractive man he is, she thought as she watched him scribble notes in the little pad.

Greg glanced at Kate again, who happened to be looking in his direction. But she turned away before he could catch her eye. "What can you tell me about Miss Armstrong?"

"We didn't talk outside of the classroom other than in student conferences, but I'll tell you what I know."

"Thank you. What do you teach?"

He turned to look at her and was bemused to find her assessing him eyes roaming over his body with interest. Embarrassed at being caught, she averted her gaze before answering "English. Brenda wanted to be a writer a novelist."

"When did the semester start?"

"In January."

"And before that, you didn't know her? She'd never taken another class with you?"

"That's right."

"Professor Helton, how long have you taught here?"

Regaining her composure, she smiled up into his eyes, but he paid no attention to her mild flirting seemed intent on asking questions and taking notes. "This is my first year."

"Was Brenda a good student?"

Annoyed that she couldn't seem to capture his interest, she followed his gaze and saw Kate standing at the bottom of the hill, seeming to be in deep discussion with Lieutenant Allen. So that's it, she thought. He's already got his eye on someone else.

"Brenda was very serious about her education."

"How was she doing in your class?"

"Well, from mid-January to sometime in March, she did great. She was a delightful student. When she walked into a room, you could feel her energy." She looked back down at the crime scene, "God, what a waste. Why anyone would want to do that to such a beautiful soul is beyond me."

"What happened in March?"

"She lost all interest in her studies. Her grade plummeted from an 'A' to a 'D'."

"Did you talk to her?"

She shrugged. "At first I thought it was just mid-semester slump. That happens sometimes, but most students snap out of it. By the time spring break rolled around in April, Brenda's performance was so bad that there was no way she'd be able to pull her grade back up she would have finished the semester with a 'D' barely."

"So, you never got the chance to talk with her?" She shook her head. "What happened after spring break?"

She swatted at an insect that flew too close to her face. "I never saw her again."

"Okay, let's go back to my original question. What makes you so sure it's Brenda Armstrong lying down there?"

"Several things."

"Such as?"

Diane sighed. "Firstly, the ring she's wearing. Her parents gave it to her last October for her birthday. Brenda loved dolphins and her parents had the ring specially made for her. In the middle is her birthstone and on each side of the stone is a dolphin nose to tail. Imbedded in each dolphin are three diamonds. The ring is platinum supposedly, there's not another one like it."

Greg shrugged, thinking it was possible that there were two rings like it and it was also possible that someone had stolen Brenda's ring either the girl down there or someone who had given it to her. "Is that it?"

"No. The watch she's wearing was a Christmas gift from her parents. It's engraved on the back: 'To our Daughter, love Mom and Dad'."

Diane reached back to remove the barrette from her hair, which tumbled around her slender shoulders. For a moment, Greg thought she was flirting again, but quickly realized she wanted him to look at the clip, not at her hair though he couldn't help but look at it too as the light played across its blonde softness.

"She bought the butterfly barrette in her hair herself. She saw mine," she held it closer so he could look at it, "and asked me where I got it. I told her at J.C. Penney's and she bought one the next day and has been wearing it since." She combed her fingers through her hair, pulled it back again and closed the barrette around it. "That is Brenda Armstrong."

"Seems like you two must have talked quite a bit in those student conferences, she ever mention having a sister or half sister?"

Diane shook her head. "No."

He raised his head, looking in Kate's direction she made a "come on" motion with her head and he rose, removing a business card from his billfold and handing it to Diane. "Thank you for your time, Professor. If you think of anything else, please don't hesitate to call me."

* * *

He rejoined Kate just as the body was being removed. "Was she any help?" Kate asked, not turning to look at her.

He touched her arm gently. "Not really. Is everything okay?"

Instead of pulling away as he half-expected, she leaned slightly toward him. "It's been a long day. I'm just tired."

He smiled down at her. "We'll be done in a few minutes." Detective Allen approached them and Greg turned his attention from the woman at his side to the other detective. "When you get the reports back, would you send me a copy? I'm interested in the caliber of the bullets and, of course, a positive ID, though I'm pretty sure it's Brenda Armstrong."

The trio began walking back up the hill toward the parking lot. "I sure will," Leroy cheerfully answered. As they reached his car, he opened the trunk to place a bag of evidence inside. "Tell you what. You keep me up to date on your case and I'll do the same with this one, deal?"

He held out his hand and Greg shook it.

"Deal, talk to you soon."

* * *

Inside his car, Greg sat for a moment, enjoying the coolness of the air conditioner and the scent of the woman at his side. "Kate, there's something I need to tell you. I don't know if this is the right time, but then, maybe there is no right time I think I'm in love with you."

"What? Have you lost your mind? We haven't known each other that long. What do you mean you think you're in love with me?" She turned her head and gazed out the side window. "Look, Greg," she said at last. "You really don't know me that well." He laid his arm along the back of her seat, leaning toward her. She could smell the musk from his body, feel his heat and felt her body responding despite her determination.

"Tell me something I don't know."

"What did the professor have to say?" she asked, changing the subject.

Greg moved his arm. "She identified the body so I took her statement."

"I know that she's very pretty."

He smiled. "Pretty, huh? Is that a little jealousy I detect? "

"No. It was just an observation."

He put the car in gear, pulled out onto the street and headed back home. "I know that 'ole green-eyed monster when I see him." He glanced at her, still smiling. "You're jealous."

"All I meant was she is a very pretty woman."

Greg shrugged as if he hadn't noticed the woman's obvious charms. "Yeah, I guess." He took one of Kate's cold hands in his. "Not as pretty as the woman sitting next to me, though."

Kate finally turned to look at him smiling back. She knew she could have Greg if she wanted him. She just wasn't sure if she could please him. Letting him hold her hand, she turned to stare out the window at the darkened landscape as they drove toward Cleveland.

"Are you going to tell Beth about Brenda's death?"

Greg sighed. "I think Dr. Hargrove should do that. Tomorrow, we can tell Chief Boswell what we found, and then he can call Dr. Hargrove and let him take it from there." They rode in silence for a while, both lost in their own thoughts.

Greg drew her fingers to his lips, kissed them softly. "Why don't you come home with me? We both need showers. I'll wash your back if you'll wash mine."

Kate jerked her hand from his grasp. Just as she was starting to get comfortable, he had to push too hard again. "I can't do that."

The smile disappeared from his face. "What happened to you Kate? Why do you freeze up at the mere mention of intimacy?"

"Greg, I told you, this is my own private hell. I'm trying to deal with it, but it takes time."

"But don't you see, Kate?" he asked softly. "You're not dealing with whatever is bothering you. You're hiding behind it. Why can't you tell me what it is?"

He waited for her response but she remained silent. Irritated by her refusal to talk, he turned the wheel and pulled over to the side of the road where he could turn to confront her. "Have you been raped?"

Kate frowned at him in disgust, unsnapped her seatbelt and slid out of the car. Greg turned the motor off and followed her. She walked a few paces away, and then turned to scream at him. "What's the matter, Greg? You know how attractive you are you're used to women falling all over you when you look down at them with those sexy green eyes, aren't you? And you can't believe that I'm not falling all over you too. Is that it?"

He stopped walking, stunned by her accusations. "That's not it and you know it."

Remaining at a safe distance, she threw back her head and laughed. "It's not? I've heard the guys in the office razzing you about all those women chasing you." Kate stepped closer to him, her dark eyes glistening in the light from the moon. "Has it ever occurred to you that maybe I'm simply not interested?"

"You're so afraid of whatever happened to you that you won't let yourself get close to me or anyone else."

Perturbed, she flung her hands into the air. He just didn't get it. He simply did not understand. She turned on her heels, stalked away and then walked back, glaring up at him as she responded through clenched teeth. "I really don't care what you think, get it? My personal life is none of your business, so let's keep it that way."

"You don't mean that."

She blinked to hold back the tears, looked up at the star-filled sky and nodded her head. "I mean it, Greg. I mean every word."

She heard the pain in his voice as he responded with a curt, "Let's go."

Neither of them spoke for the remainder of the trip and when he pulled into the parking lot in front of her apartment, he simply stared out through the windshield, waiting for her to leave the car.

She opened the door and hesitated for a moment before turning back toward him. "You're like an open book waiting for anyone that passes by to read it. I wish I was more like that, but I've closed myself inside this cocoon I can't get out and no one can get in."

He watched her his desire to speak, to respond in some way was evident in his eyes, but he kept silent, listening with interest. "But, you are right about one thing. I do care about you and it scares the hell out of me.

"If I tell myself long enough that I don't care, eventually I won't," she smiled.

"You'll get tired of waiting for me, Greg, and you'll find an intelligent, beautiful woman and fall in love with her—the best part is that she'll love you right back and me? I'll still be inside my cocoon where I know I'll be safe."

"I won't let that happen, Kate."

She leaned toward him, took his hand between both of hers and held it to her cheek for a moment. A single tear escaped from the corner of her eye and ran unchecked down her face. "You don't have a choice. All my secrets are locked inside this cocoon with me and I don't share them with anyone." She squeezed his hand once before releasing it, then turned and exited the vehicle.

Greg could only watch as she entered her apartment, waiting for her to turn on the lights before driving away hurt and disappointment planting firm little feet in his chest, making themselves right at home.

Chapter Twenty-One

Kate undressed and slipped into a short cotton robe before starting the water in the bathtub and pouring in scented bubble bath. The heady aroma of jasmine filled the air and she could feel the steam beginning to ease the tension of the day even before she removed the robe and sank into the water. Rolling a small towel, she placed it behind her neck and lay back against the bathtub with her eyes closed.

Memories of the day filled her mind and Greg seemed to be a part of each of them. Images of him smiling, bending down to examine the body in Athens, looking at her with concern and then anger, and finally hurt swirled behind her closed eyelids and—the cell phone she'd dropped on the rug beside the tub rang insistently. Should I answer or let it ring until the caller decided to hang up, she wondered? Answer, she told herself as she stretched out a slender arm to pick it up.

"Hello?"

"Are you all right?" a familiar voice asked.

She sat up a bit straighter, feeling a surge of relief at her decision to answer the phone. "You're home already?"

He chuckled. "No, I'm in the car cell phone. What are you doing?"

"I'm soaking in a tub of bubbles."

He hesitated for a moment as he thought of her lithe, naked form submerged in a tub full of bubbles. "I don't want to scare you away, Kate, but I am so attracted to you. Please don't shut me out."

"I think I'm falling for you, too. Isn't it strange that I can tell you on the phone what I can't say to your face? But there's so many things you still don't know about me."

Greg struggled to find the words that would give her the reassurance she needed. "Kate, let's try again. I promise I won't pressure you. We can take things as slowly as you need?"

"It may take a while."

He breathed a sigh of relief. "As long as I'm with you, I don't care how long it takes. Do you want to get together tomorrow night?"

She smiled, closing her eyes as she listened to the sound of his voice felt the patience and love behind his words. "Okay."

Turning into his driveway, Greg turned off the motor and pulled the key from the ignition. "I'd better go get some rest. I'll see you in the morning."

"In the morning," she repeated. "Good night."

She pressed the talk button to disconnect the call and dropped the phone back to the rug before sliding further down into the water with a smile of anticipation playing across her lips. Her pleasure suddenly dissipated as she sensed the presence of something someone in the room. Her eyes flew open and her heart began to pound crazily as she opened her eyes to see a man looming over her. She tried to stand, to scramble out of the tub but his hands were already on her shoulders, forcing her head under the water holding her there with ease even though she struggled and kicked against him. Just as she thought her lungs must surely burst from the lack of air, he grabbed a handful of her hair and jerked. She came up gasping and coughing.

Just as she was starting to draw a deep breath, he shoved her under again where she splashed and fought to no avail. He yanked her up again, and then plunged her back her struggles grew weaker my God, she thought. I'm dying. No! And she found the strength to push herself upward a final time. He backed away as she leaned over the edge of the tub, coughing and spitting out water. Her chest ached, her lungs burned, but she was still alive.

He grabbed a handful of hair and pulled her upward until her face was mere inches from his. "Can you hear me, Kate?" He shook her roughly by the hair and she nodded in response. "Good. Now pay attention. Mr. Westmoreland is very unhappy with you. He was mad enough when he had to get me to take care of the Armstrong's and now this.

"He sent me to give you a message. If that partner of yours starts getting too close to be on the verge of solving this, you're to take him out. Or, I'll take both of you out." Letting go of her hair, he shoved her back into the water and got to his feet. He turned and slipped away into the night as quietly as he had come

Crying, choking, gagging, Kate tried to pull herself over the edge of the tub, but her feet kept slipping. Finally managing to get up on her knees, she heaved herself out and lay gasping on the water-soaked rug. "Get out of here, Kate", she said. "He may still be in the apartment." Rolling onto her stomach, she began to half-crawl, half drag herself from the room but stopped as she began to cough and retch again water spewed from her mouth as her stomach heaved. Finally, after what seemed like hours, she could draw in several, short gasping breaths and felt her lungs slowly began to fill and the strength return to her arms and legs. She grabbed for a bath towel, wrapped it around herself as she rose to her feet, and collapsed onto the closed toilet seat where she sat for long moments simply breathing in huge lungful of life-giving air.

A dream, she thought incoherently. It must be a bad dream and I'll wake up any moment safe and dry in my own bed. No. She jerked her head up and looked around the room. Where was he? Rising shakily to her feet, she stumbled down the hallway and into the living room. The front door stood open to the night air, but she sensed that he was gone. Crossing the room, she grabbed a chair from in front of the table and dragged it behind her as she approached the door. Slamming and locking it, she wedged the chair under the knob for good measure before collapsing onto the floor still struggling to draw in a deep breath.

As she leaned against the door, she looked around the room the closet door was wide open and she felt her heart began to race again as she slowly got to her feet and crossed the room. She dropped to her knees in front of the door and didn't even notice the towel slipping to the floor as she spied a familiar box inside the closet. It was the box with the gun and silencer she'd mailed back to Westmoreland. Is that what the man who'd tried to drown her been sent to do? Retrieving the towel, she stood and slowly crossed the room to collapse onto the couch. She had to get those things out of here fast. What if Greg were to find them? Or worse what if they could link her to a crime?

I'm so tired she thought so incredibly tired. I'll deal with it later. And still coughing, she leaned against the back of the couch and closed her eyes

* * *

Bright and early the next morning, Greg and Boswell sat drinking coffee together in the chief's office as they waited for a delivery from GBI.

"Here they come" Greg announced unnecessarily as they turned to watch two men in coveralls enter the police station, carrying a heavy box between them.

"This is everything we found in the trunk of the car," the taller of the two announced as Boswell and Greg stepped out to meet them. "We followed normal procedure took fingerprints, vacuumed the front and back floorboards, front and back seats, and the trunk. Everything's labeled and we're taking all of it to the crime lab. The car is pretty clean no visible evidence of a crime, we'll see though."

Chief Boswell nodded and shook hands with both men, who immediately turned to leave. "Thanks, fellows."

Greg sat on the edge of the desk and peered into the box. The diaries Beth had told him about lay among a scattering of other papers and he picked one up and opened it. "Look at this. It's in a child's handwriting, just like Beth said." Greg handed it to Boswell as he reached for another, but stopped and looked up when he heard someone coughing it was Kate.

He excused himself for a moment and crossed the room to greet her. "You want to have lunch with me today?"

She smiled. "Sure, but I need to take a rain check on tonight."

"Is something wrong?"

"No. I think I caught a chest cold last night. I don't think it would be much fun for you if I spent the evening coughing all over you."

"Lunch around eleven?"

"Sure." Greg returned to the chief and the box while Kate tried to look busy. But the horror of last night was still too fresh in her mind the nightmarish images kept running through her head. Had the man known her? Had he been stalking her? She'd only lived in Cleveland for a few weeks and hadn't met many people and most of them were police officers. Was he one of them?

Someone touched her arm and she jumped a bit, startled at the touch. It was Greg. "Come on. Let's get out of here for a while."

He opened the passenger door for her before going around to the other side and sliding in under the wheel. "I'm not making a fool of myself, am I?" he asked.

She grinned. "Well, if you are, I hope you don't stop. Where are we going?"

"I want to show you a very romantic spot."

Greg turned off the main road onto an unused dirt path and pulled into a clearing that could have been lifted directly from a Currier and Ives print. An old mill, it's wheel long silent, stood next to a stream that tumbled and laughed its way over small boulders and rocks to create a waterfall, which ended in a pool where Kate actually saw two fish leap above the water's surface as she stared mesmerized by the beauty of the scene.

Several of the rocks from the wall running alongside the building had toppled to the ground where an abundance of wild flowers had sprung up between and around them. And although she could not see them beneath the overgrowth of weeds and saplings, Kate knew that the ruts made by the wheels of hundreds of wagons pulled by patient mules and horses as they carried load after load of grain to the mill were still there she thought if she listened hard enough she just might be able to catch an echo of hooves and the soft neigh of an animal as it stood in line, waiting for its turn to move forward.

Kate was flattered beyond words to know that Greg was willing to share this private sanctuary with her and she smiled at him as he came around the car to open her door and hold her hand as she stepped into the cool air created by shade of overhanging trees and the water.

"It's beautiful," she whispered

Greg smiled as he led her to the rock wall where they could stare down at the gurgling stream. "I can't get you out of my mind, Kate. When I'm with you, I want to be closer. When we're not together, I'm miserable. Is that love?

She shook her head. "Greg, you don't know me."

"But I want too if you'll tell me."

"You wouldn't like what you'd hear."

Placing his hands on both sides of her face, Greg tilted her head so he could stare into her eyes. "Why don't you tell me and let me determine my own reaction?" Her eyes locked on his as he bent forward, intent on kissing her soft, full lips, but a sudden fit of coughing overtook her and she turned away, covering her mouth with her hands.

"Damn it," Greg moaned in frustration. "What's wrong?"

She leaned back against the wall, head down as she tried to catch her breath. "I told you—I seem to have come down with a chest cold, but it will clear up in a day or two."

"I'm sorry, Kate. You sound miserable let's get back in the car. We can do this another time." She smiled grateful for his patience and understanding, and then let him put his arm around her shoulders as they walked back to the car.

Chapter Twenty-Two

When he left the station for the day, Greg took Beth's diaries with him. He began reading the first one as he sat at the table eating a solitary dinner of canned soup and stale crackers. Determined to keep reading after he ate, he settled into the recliner where he immediately drifted off to sleep only to be awakened a short time later by the insistent ringing of the telephone. He answered, still groggy from his nap, but came instantly awake when he recognized George Cutler's voice on the other end.

"Mr. Cutler, George, thanks for returning my call."

"I'm sorry to call so late but your call sounded urgent. I've been out of town for the last few days and just got in. Is there something you need from me?"

Greg glanced at the clock—eleven-thirty, so much for spending the evening reading. "Yeah, I have a question for you. Were the police report and photos of the car explosion in the envelope you found with your mother's things?"

"No, I got those copies myself. Why?"

"Did you read the report?"

"Yes, of course. Is there a problem with it?"

Rising from the comfort of the recliner, Greg crossed the room to remove the file from his briefcase and spread the information across the dining room table. "You're an engineer, what do you think? Do you believe the car exploded because of a mechanical failure?"

"I asked the officer who gave me the report the same thing. He explained that the accident happened twenty years ago when they didn't have the technology available to determine the exact cause of the explosion that would be available today."

"Do you remember the officer's name?"

"Sure. It was Goodwin."

Greg stared at the name at the bottom of

the original police report. "Carl Goodwin?"

"Yes."

"How old do you think he is?"

"I'd say he's in his mid-sixties or so why are you interested in him?"

Greg ignored the question for the moment "Was he in uniform or was he a plain-clothes detective?"

"Uniform? I'll ask you again why are you so interested in him?"

"Because twenty years ago the <u>detective</u> in charge of the investigation was Carl Goodwin," Greg told him.

"Hold on a minute," George said and Greg could hear the rustling of papers in the background before the other man came back on the line. "I'll be damned! Why didn't I notice that before? No wonder he fed me such a line of bullshit—he was covering his own ass. I'm going down there in the morning to file a complaint."

"You can't do that. Not just yet anyway."

"Can you give me one goddamn reason why I can't?"

"Because I think Goodwin is up to his eyebrows in this whole mess—the deaths of the Armstrong's as well as the killing of your brother." I have to tell him about Brenda too, he thought. "George, are you sitting down?"

He heard the scrape of a chair leg against tile and could almost see the other man seating himself at the table in his spotless kitchen. "I am now. Do you have more bad news?"

"Yes, I'm sorry. But I've got some good news too." He heard George's sharp intake of breath before he asked for the bad news first. "Brenda Armstrong—or the young woman known to you as Tammy Cutler, was murdered." Greg paused when he heard George drop the phone and a woman's voice—he assumed it must be George's wife, asking, "What's wrong? What's wrong?" And then he heard a man's sobs and word of comfort from the woman. Just as he thought he should hang up and let George call him back later, the other man picked up the phone again.

"She was the only link to my brother I had. Now I have nothing. Why did they have to kill her?"

Greg could offer no explanation and didn't even try. "Do you remember talking about the girl in the hospital? The one I told you is Tammy's half-sister? Her name is Bethany Akin and she is also your brother's child. David had a yearlong affair with her mother, Suzanne Akin, who got pregnant with Bethany.

"David ended the affair just before he and Carol married and he didn't know about Bethany then. He didn't find out about the little girl until her mother, Suzanne, came down with ovarian cancer when Bethany was two and a half.

"She was terrified that when she died Bethany would be placed in an orphanage because she had no other family to take in the child. She contacted David, they met and discussed Bethany. Suzanne was taking your brother to meet his child when the car exploded—she was the woman he was with, not your sister-in-law Carol."

"My God," George said. "Do you believe this story?"

Greg placed the girl's college pictures side by side as he responded. "I think I told you that Bethany—who likes to be called Beth, by the way, could pass for Tammy's twin. Beth has been attending college at the University of Virginia and says she just found out about Tammy last January.

"I'm planning to come back up there and I want to bring a Detective Leroy Allen from Athens with me—he's the one investigating your niece's murder. I'll talk to him and to my boss in the morning and hopefully we'll be up there the first of next week. If you go to the police station to file a complaint, you'll alert Goodwin and I'd really like to pay him a surprise visit."

George sighed heavily. "Detective, I trust you and I think you're trying to do the right thing so I'll keep quiet. When do you think I could meet Beth?"

"When Detective Allen and I finish our work up there, you can come down to see her. But right now, I want her to stay put—I think she's safe in the hospital."

* * *

Even though the next day was Saturday, Greg went into the office and was both pleased and surprised to see Kate already at her desk, "you feeling okay this morning?"

"Sorry about canceling last night. And yes, I'm much better this morning. Thank you."

"That's okay we'll make it another time. You look tired, Kate. Did you get any sleep last night?"

She looked up at him for a moment, and then quickly turned her head so he wouldn't see the sudden rush of tears in her eyes "A little."

Boswell's door swung open and he stuck his head out into the common room. "Greg," he bellowed when he spotted the detective. "I want you in here right now!" He glared as Greg entered the office and he slammed the door behind the detective.

"What did I do?" Greg asked.

Seated behind his desk, Boswell looked up at Greg, and then nodded his head in the direction of the door, meaning he wanted to know what was up with Kate. Greg shrugged without comment—he had no intentions of sharing their private lives at this point. Boswell let it drop.

"Did you get a phone call from Beatrice Langston the other night?"

"Yeah how do you know? You got my phones bugged or something?" Greg asked as he sat in one of the chairs facing Boswell's desk.

"What? No, of course not I got a call from her last night too and she told me she'd talked with you. So, what are you gonna do?"

Rising, Greg began to pace around the room. He always felt as if his thoughts were clearer if he could move around. "I want to meet with Leroy Allen and ask him to go to Quincy with me. The answers to all of our questions, including who murdered the Armstrong's, are up there."

Boswell listened, nodding his agreement, and then got to his feet and moved toward the door. Placing his hand on the doorknob, he turned to Greg with a grin on his face. "Just to make this look real for anyone who wants to think you're in serious trouble, I'm gonna yell at ya."

"Are you planning to hurt my feelings?"

Boswell's grin grew even wider as he flung the door open with a bang and motioned Greg out who was happy to play along, scurried out, head down as if shamed by his bad behavior.

"Don't you come back in here until you get your shit together! You hear me, Garrison?" Boswell yelled.

Greg grabbed his briefcase and turned to Boswell. "I've got my shit together. You're the one that don't know his ass from a hole in the ground!"

Boswell's mouth flew open before he pointed in the direction of the front entrance. "Get out of here!"

Greg didn't trust himself to say anything else. The laugh he was suppressing wasn't going to stay back much longer. He rushed from the building and leaned against his car chuckling as he thought about the shocked expression on the chief's face—that had been a real Kodak moment if there ever was one.

* * *

Greg waited until he was beyond the mountain range around Cleveland before placing a call to Leroy Allen to ask if he had time to meet. Leroy agreed before informing Greg that the gun used in the other murders was also the one that killed Brenda Armstrong. Greg whooped and hollered, congratulating Leroy as if he'd performed a miracle. His enthusiasm was contagious and Leroy laughed heartily while he tried to explain to Greg that he hadn't done a thing––he wasn't the one who did the forensic testing on the bullet, but Greg didn't care. He was thrilled that everything was starting to fall into place at last. After Greg calmed down, they agreed on a place to meet in Athens and ended the conversation.

Greg hummed along with the country song blaring from his speakers. Some good-old-boy was singing about how amazing the woman in his life was and Greg's thoughts automatically turned to Kate. He focused on the way she'd looked when they'd driven out to the old mill—eyes shining at the beauty of their surroundings, the fall of her hair across her cheek, so silky soft that he wanted to bury his hands in it as her full, kissable mouth turned up to his, waiting wanting the feel of his lips against hers. And then another song started something about hold me tight, let's close the door and make love tonight, and Greg gave himself a mental shake. No time to go <u>there</u> right now. There was work to be done and it needed his full attention. He'd have time to think about beautiful, intelligent Kate later, but right now he needed to talk with Leroy and set up the trip to Quincy.

It was almost noon when Greg merged into the heavy traffic around Georgia Mall. Driving through the parking lot, he spotted Leroy waiting for him at one of the mall's many entrances he honked to get his attention, waved when the other man glanced up at him, and then indicated he'd meet him as soon as he found a place to park, which, unfortunately, turned out to be at least a quarter of a mile away.

When he stepped out of the car, the afternoon heat smashed into him like a ball of fire and he was glad for the tennis shoes on his feet that made jogging back toward the mall entrance that much easier. Leroy was still waiting in the same place, looking cool and collected in his Brooks Brother's suit while Greg felt rivulets of sweat pooling under his arms and around the waistband of his jeans. "Inside," he panted and Leroy followed him into the noisy coolness of the mall.

Greg watched in awe as Leroy glided his way toward the food court while he trudged along beside him tennis shoes squeaking on the freshly waxed floor. This guy is beyond cool, he thought as they ordered drinks and found a table amidst the usual mall crowd of teenage girls with too much makeup, boy's dressed in low-slung jeans and baggy tee shirts and harried mothers with small children in tow nothing new here.

They exchanged small talk for a few minutes and Leroy asked about Kate. Something in Greg's expression must have changed because the other man immediately held up a hand in apology. "Sorry, man," he said. "I didn't know the lady was spoken for."

"Actually, I don't know if she is or not, but I hope so."

"Good luck there, my man. Now let's get down to business." Greg provided the other detective with some background information before telling him about the call from Beatrice Langston, and then they planned their strategy with Greg cautioning Leroy several times not to discuss anything with anyone but his boss. They would take the earliest flight to Boston on the following Monday morning and would pay a visit to Carl Goodwin as soon as possible. Satisfied with their plan, they finished lunch and headed back out into the afternoon heat where Greg began to sweat immediately and Leroy still looked dazzling the man's a cucumber Greg thought as they went their separate ways after promising to meet at the

Atlanta airport bright and early Monday morning.

Driving back toward Cleveland, Greg impulsively decided to give Kate a call. She answered on the first ring. "Hey, there," he said by way of greeting.

"Greg. I'm so glad it's you."

The joy in her voice sent a finger of excitement down his spine, but he also sensed something else there. Was it fear? "Is something wrong?"

"No just happy to hear a friendly voice."

"You up to company tonight?"

She hesitated for a moment and Greg drew in a deep breath as he waited for the usual thanks but no thanks response. "Sure," she said instead. "I'd love that."

"Great! See you around seven."

It was around five-thirty when he pulled into his driveway with thoughts of Kate still running through his head. It was obvious that something was bothering her and he hoped she'd finally break down and tell him about it tonight. He went inside, heading straight for the shower. As he stepped from beneath the cool spray, he heard the chiming of the doorbell and quickly dried and donned a pair of shorts to hurry to the door.

Kate stood on the porch, thumb pressed against the doorbell even after he opened the door. "Do you mind?" she asked as she burst into tears.

Gently removing her thumb from the doorbell, he led her into the den where he sat with her on the couch. "Of course I don't mind. What's wrong?"

"I'm so frightened, Greg. I just couldn't stay home."

He pulled her against his chest where the steady thump-thump of his heart began to calm her frazzled nerves. "What are you afraid of?"

She leaned closer as if trying to draw strength from his touch. "Remember when you called the other night and I was taking a bubble bath?" She didn't wait for his response. "When we hung up there was a . . . a . . . a man was in my apartment, Greg. He tried to drown me I was so scared. I honestly thought I was about to die. I would have died if he hadn't let me go." She burst into fresh tears at the memory of the stranger in her house at the thought of his threats and almost wished she hadn't come here. Almost, but she needed Greg, needed his warmth and the comfort of his arms around her like they were now.

Knowing instinctively that it had not been a random act of violence, Greg tried to remain calm even as he felt the urge to cause someone great pain threatening to override his good sense. He knew his earlier fears about Kate's safety were right and he needed to find out what was happening before he could help her. "What kind of trouble are you in, Kate?"

She looked up into his eyes wanting him to hold her like this forever, but she knew that wasn't possible. Gently extracting herself from his arms, she leaned against the back of the couch. "My troubles started when I was twelve. How much time do you have?"

He leaned over and kissed her gently. "All the time in the world," he whispered as he looked deep into her exhausted eyes. He kissed her again. "Did you get any sleep last night?"

She yawned loudly. "What little I got was while I was sitting on the couch I couldn't stop coughing. It felt like my lungs were still full of water."

Feeling safer than she had in a long time, Kate closed her eyes and immediately dropped off to sleep. Greg left the room only long enough to turn back the covers on his bed, and then came back to scoop her slender frame up into his arms. Her eyelids fluttered and she gasped.

"It's okay," he whispered against the cup of her ear. "I'm putting you to bed.

We'll talk in the morning."

He wanted her to be comfortable and didn't think she would be dressed in the clothes she'd worn to work that morning. Taking a tee shirt from his dresser, he stood looking down at her for a moment. How am I supposed to do this, he wondered, and then shrugged. "What the hell," he said aloud as he undressed her down to her underwear and slipped the large tee shirt over her head she didn't resist, wasn't even aware of his presence. He pulled the sheet up over her, then turned and left the room.

After he'd eaten, he sat at the kitchen table getting his notes in order. He thought he heard a cry and jumped up to rush into the bedroom. Kate was still sleeping, but she was struggling against some unseen enemy and gasping for breath. Switching on the bedside lamp, he sat next to her and shook her shoulder. "Wake up, Kate. Wake up," he whispered so as not to startle her.

Her terror-filled eyes flew open and she struggled against him for a moment. "It's only me, Kate. You're okay." Coming fully awake, she recognized him, grabbed his shoulders and pulled him down against her trembling body.

Greg kissed the top of her head, put his arms around her and rocked her like a child. "It was only a dream." From her position on the pillow, she looked up at him and nodded.

He stood, straightening the twisted sheet and pulling it back up over her. She bolted upright, dark eyes filling with terror once more. "Don't leave me. Please, don't leave me."

He smiled and shook his head. "I'm not leaving you. I'll be in the next room."

Reaching out, she grasped his hand and pulled him back to the bed. "No. Don't leave me alone!"

Walking around to the other side of the bed, he stretched out beside her. "Is this better?"

She nodded as she scooted across the

bed to rest her head against his broad, shirtless chest. Wrapping his arms around her, he closed his eyes and inhaled the sweet aroma of her hair. He felt her relax and knew she'd fallen back to sleep. He tried to extract himself, to get up but she wrapped her arms tightly around his waist, holding him close. Slowly opening her eyes again, she stared up at him as her fingers moved across his chest. Pulling her up so that she lay across him, he kissed her and without any hesitation she kissed back, grinding her slender hips against his.

He couldn't remember if she'd removed her tee shirt or if he had but it was on the floor in a crumpled heap. He was unfastening her bra with shaking hands when he cupped her small breasts in his hands, a wave of desire unlike any other swept over him. He couldn't remember wanting another woman as much as he wanted her right here and right now.

Neither of them spoke as they stared into one another's eyes. Greg's hands roamed over her body as they began to exchange heat-filled kisses. He rolled her onto her back, propping himself on his elbows as he continued to kiss and caress her. She moaned against his lips as he attempted to enter her his hardness against her thigh both aroused and terrified her and she tensed a little.

Wanting her, needing her, Greg sensed her fear and pulled away a little even though the yearning to plunge into her soft warmth was almost overwhelming. "Is this your first time," he asked, the words slurred by desire.

"Yes," she whispered. "But don't stop. Please don't stop."

He kissed her lips slowly, tenderly moved away from her mouth to plant feathery kisses down the side of her neck and gently took first one hard nipple and then the other into his mouth. She moaned, her hands came up around his neck to pull him closer, closer and he began to suck greedily as he reached between her now spread thighs to rub and tickle before carefully pressing his hardness into her waiting, willing body. She rose to meet him and he moaned his own pleasure. No matter what happens, he thought, I love this woman I will do anything to keep her safe, and then all coherent thought left him as he made slow, tender love to her, taking her up and away from her body to a place she had never imagined. At that moment Kate knew that as long as Greg was at her side, nothing or no one would ever hurt her again.

When the lovemaking was over and they lay replete in a tangle of arms and legs upon the crumpled sheets, Greg brushed the sweaty hair from her forehead and kissed her softly. "You okay?" he whispered, already feeling slumber's sweet embrace reaching out to claim him.

She smiled drowsily and rubbed a hand across his chest. "Yes," she whispered back and they drifted off into dreamless sleep together.

Greg was showered and dressed in a pair of khaki shorts and a white tee shirt with coffee brewing. He had spread a fresh onion bagel with cream cheese when Kate wandered into the kitchen redressed in his oversized tee shirt. It was apparent that she wore nothing underneath when she raised her arms over her head to stretch and yawn loudly. Smiling, Greg enjoyed the view for a moment before offering her coffee and a section of the newspaper he was preparing to read.

She pulled out a chair on the other side of the table and sat down, smiling at him sleepily. "You all right," he asked and she blushed under his gaze.

"Much better, thank you," she said almost primly, and then they both burst into gales of laughter as they stared at one another across the tabletop.

He stood to get another cup from the cabinet and poured in just a dollop of cream before adding the coffee.

"How'd you know I like cream in my coffee?"

"Because I can't keep my eyes off you, I see every move you make, from pouring in the cream before filling the cup with coffee to that little frown line right there between your eyebrows," he touched his own forehead to show her the exact spot, "when you don't get your own way." Coming back to the table, he sat the full cup in front of her, and then leaned forward to plant a tender kiss upon her slightly swollen lips. "Last night was wonderful."

She stared at him for a long moment before silently mouthing his name and he kissed her again, cupping her chin in his hand for a moment before sitting back in his chair with a serious expression on his handsome face. "Kate I want to know about the trouble you're in."

She pulled on her tee shirt, avoiding his gaze for a moment. "Can I take a shower first?"

"Sure," he smiled reassuringly at her. "I'm feeling generous this morning. But then I expect you to sit your pretty little butt back down in that chair and tell me everything."

Chapter Twenty-Three

Freshly showered, Kate returned to the kitchen dressed in the outfit she'd worn the day before. She sat at the table, fidgeting like a schoolgirl who'd gotten caught cheating on an exam. She chewed nervously on a fingernail as she watched Greg watching her.

"Where do you want me to start?"

He came around the table to sit next to her, taking both of her hands between his, he smiled reassuringly. "Last night you said your troubles started when you were twelve. That sounds like a good place to start."

"I can't tell you about that. No one knows except my mother." She jumped from the chair and started for the door.

Greg followed her into the living room, grabbed her arm and pulled her back into an embrace as she struggled for a moment before collapsing against his broad chest. "What happened, Kate? If you can tell anyone, it's me."

She trembled as the memory washed over her. "Why do you think I've never had sex before last night?"

He held her tighter for a moment, dreading what he was about to hear but knowing she needed to talk if she was ever to move past it. "Tell me, Kate."

"Don't make me do this," she pleaded.

"Kate, listen to me. I cannot make you do anything but it's obvious that whatever happened still has control over you. Talking about it will help put you back in charge of your life, it's time, Kate."

She pushed away from him, wandering around the room to pick up an object here and there before settling on the couch where she stared down at her hands. "I have an older sister. Her name is Margaret, Margie for short. She's seven years older than me and she's always been a mama's girl. After she got married, she'd make her husband drive her back home every other weekend.

"My parents thought he was the greatest

thing in the world I was twelve and they were spending the weekend. My parents' room was next to mine, and Margie and her husband had her old room down the hall. Everyone was sleeping everyone except . . ." Hot tears began to roll unchecked down her face and she hugged herself tightly as she rocked back and forth on the couch.

"He came into my room the sound of a floorboard squeaking or something that shouldn't have been there woke me. I saw a shadowy figure crossing the room toward my bed. I was so scared I started to call out for Daddy, but it was too late. He was on top of me with a hand over my mouth and nose so I couldn't scream could barely breathe. I fought him the best I could, but I was a little girl and he was so big, so strong. He raped me, in my own bed, in my own room. And nobody was there to stop him nobody there to help me."

Burying her face in her hands, she sobbed like a child and Greg thought his heart would surely break if she didn't stop. He wanted to go to her, to gather her in his arms and whisper words of comfort into her ear but he knew if he touched her at that moment, she would bolt be out the door faster than he could get up and follow. So he waited. After a few minutes, she drew a deep breath, wiped her nose on the back of her hand and shook her head.

"The next morning, still dressed in the same nightgown now covered in my own blood, I went to find my mother. I wanted her to hold me, to tell me everything would be okay, but when I told her what happened, she didn't say a word. She just turned me around and started pushing me back up the stairs I was stumbling, crying, but she just kept pushing until we were in the bathroom and she could slam and lock the door so no one could see us see my shame.

"I stood there shivering in humiliation and pain when she pulled the nightgown off over my head and turned to fill the tub to wash away the evidence. Finally, after she shoved me into the too hot water and put a washcloth and a bar of soap in my hands, she spoke to me."

She looked at Greg, the pain of the memory fresh in her eyes. "Want to know what she said to me?"

"What, honey?"

"It's just one of those things that happens in families sometimes." She laughed, but it was an ugly, harsh sound full of anger and pain. "I told her I wanted to tell Daddy wanted him to make it all better. She said, 'Katie, you know your father's a busy man. And what can he do about it now?'

"I remember just staring at her thinking she didn't really mean it. Daddy could make everything better. That was his job.

"Suddenly she was very angry at me. She jerked me out of the tub and started rubbing me with a towel hard. It hurt and I started to cry again. She grabbed me by the shoulders and shook me. 'Stop being a baby and listen to me,' she said. 'If word ever gets out that you had sex with your brother-in-law your sister's husband, for God's sake and at your age, the family will be disgraced and your daddy will have to quit his job with the police force.'"

She looked at Greg, confusion and anger mingling in her dark eyes. "He raped me and she called it sex I was violated, humiliated and hurt beyond words, but all she worried about was the goddamn family name! I wanted comfort and protection and all I got was a hot bath and a scolding"

And then he did rise, crossing the room at last to sit beside her on the couch and put his arms around her to wipe the tears from her cheeks and kiss her forehead, her hair and closed eyelids. "Why didn't you tell your father anyway?"

"What do you think he'd have done?"

"He was a policeman your father, and he would have arrested the bastard."

She shook her head in disagreement,

pushed herself up from the couch and crossed the room, turning to stare at him. "He was next in line to become Chief of Police. You have no idea what that meant to my parents. If I told Dad, my mother would have convinced him that it was my fault." She shrugged "Same outcome, more pain."

"Kate, a rape test would have proven differently."

She laughed at his naiveté. "I was twelve years old, a minor. My parents had all the control." She sighed heavily, moving across the room to touch a figurine on the mantelpiece. "I felt so hopeless, so trapped and alone. I knew no one would listen to me not when my father, a high-ranking police officer, was willing to call me a liar in front of the whole world.

"So I locked it away inside, just like I locked my bedroom door every time Margie and Derrick came to spend the weekend. From that day on, I did the opposite of everything my parents wanted me to do.

"I ran with a very rough crowd. I never used any of the drugs that circulated so freely and I certainly never let a man touch me." She crossed the room again to stand in front of him. "I never wanted anyone to touch me. Until last night, that is." He reached for her, the sympathy for her heartache clear on his face, but she turned away.

"Anyway, I finished high school, even made the honor roll. And then I started working for the Clarke County Police Department, but I still ran with a rough crowd.

"I was with them when they picked up drugs and sold them, and even when they counted their drug money all because I knew my parents wouldn't approve.

"When you run with a rough crowd, sooner or later, you're bound to get your hands dirty." She crossed the room again, this time stopping in front of the bay window where she could stare out at the yard and the street beyond.

"A couple of months ago, I was at a party where drugs were floating around pretty freely. A strange man approached me, introducing himself as Mr. Westmoreland. He said he had something he wanted me to take care for him. I laughed in his face, told him I wasn't one of his drug people and he got angry.

"He told me he had photos and videotapes of me with his people when they made their buys and sales. He said he even had pictures of me with them counting money if I didn't do what he wanted, copies of everything would be mailed to my father and to the DA's office." She turned to look at Greg who had gotten to his feet and was staring at her with a scowl on his face.

"Westmoreland's the one who told me to come up here and apply for the detective position. In the last week of May, I got a letter from him. When I opened the envelope, five one thousand-dollar bills dropped out. There was a note saying I should expect to receive a package soon it came the next day.

Inside, there was a nine-millimeter, complete with silencer and a box of 123 grain cartridges. A few minutes after the package arrived, he phoned me." She paused as she looked into Greg's troubled eyes.

"He said there was a problem here in Cleveland he wanted me to take care. I wanted to know what kind of problem it was. He said twenty years ago a man named Philip Sharply disappeared taking twenty million dollars with him it belonged to Westmoreland. Sharply was now living in Cleveland under the name of Joseph Armstrong Westmoreland wanted me to take this man and his family out."

All sympathy gone, Greg crossed the room in long strides, grabbing her by the shoulders and shaking her. "What the hell are you saying? Are you the killer?"

Shaking off his grasp, she shook her head. "No, I refused. I mailed the gun and the money to a drop box in Maryland."

"The other night when that man broke in . . ." she stopped, interrupting her own train of thought. "I think he was wearing a disguise, Greg. He told me Westmoreland was disappointed with me and he was the one who'd had to take care of the Armstrong's.

"He warned me that if my partner meaning you, got too close to finding out the truth, I was to take him out. If I didn't, he'd take us both out."

Angry almost beyond words, Greg stared at her, unable to believe she'd kept something so important from him. "Why didn't you tell me before now?"

"I knew I was falling in love with you and I didn't want to lose you." When he showed no reaction, she continued. "I think the man who broke in planted the gun, possibly the knife, and the money in my apartment."

He shook his head in disgust. "Are you telling me those things are in your apartment right now?"

She shrugged. "I'm not sure. There's a box that looks like the one I returned sitting on the floor in my closet. I haven't opened it yet. I was too afraid."

"I'm calling Chief Boswell and you're gonna tell him exactly what you just told me. Then, we're taking the box and its contents down to the station for fingerprinting," he said as he crossed the room to pick up the phone.

"Greg, I haven't told you everything yet."

Hesitating for a moment, he finally nodded, and then replaced the phone and paced from the den into the kitchen and back. "Don't tell me anything else. Not another word. I don't care how much I love you I refuse to become an accessory." He glared at her, picked up the phone again and started to dial Boswell's number.

She gently took the phone from his hand and hung it up. "I'm not alone in this I'm working with the FBI."

"What the hell are you talking about now?"

"After Westmoreland talked to me at the party, I called the F.B.I to see if they had anything on him. They've been after him for years, but could never get enough evidence to make charges stick. They're the reason I came here and took the job not Westmoreland."

She stared up into his face. "Someone in your department is crooked, but I don't know who it is yet." He didn't respond so she continued with her story. "Anyway, they put a tap on my phone, but they never expected Westmoreland to come here but he did. The Saturday morning of the murders, Westmoreland and one of his henchmen paid me an unexpected visit. I was forced at gunpoint to go with them to Armstrong's office Beatrice Langston was there.

"When we burst through the door, I could tell by the expression on her face that she knew Westmoreland clearly, she was afraid for her life. She was at her desk counting a pile of money. Westmoreland's henchman had come in with a duffel bag and he simply crossed the room and raked all of the money into the bag before Westmoreland forced Miss Langston to leave with him, which left me alone with the other guy." She glanced at Greg, trying to gauge his reaction. He seemed to be listening but made no attempt to interrupt. She couldn't tell whether he was paying attention or if he was trying to come up with a quick solution to the problem.

"After a while, they returned Langston was visibly shaken. Westmoreland told me he was leaving her with me and this time I'd better take care of business, or else. They left and I asked her where he'd taken her. She said they'd gone to the bank where she'd transferred all the money from Armstrong's account to one of Westmoreland's."

Kate paused, rubbing her forehead in an attempt to ease the pounding behind her temples. It didn't help. "She said Westmoreland told her that small town cops were easy to buy they worked cheap. I didn't understand and asked her to explain. She started to cry then it was awful. She sobbed and sobbed, but finally managed to get herself under control. Then she told me Joseph and Bette Armstrong had just been murdered and the killer was a police office." Unable to bear the disgust in his eyes, she turned away.

"I called the FBI from her office and they spoke with both of us. They instructed me to let her go because she had documented records on some key people they were after. They also informed me she would only give them what they needed after they let her go. Sort of a, quid pro quo thing do, this for me and I'll do this for you." She moved slowly toward him.

"I admit that I've done some pretty stupid things like running with the bad guys, but I'm not into drugs and I'm not a killer. I'm a cop. I've already given their names to the F.B.I, and when the time comes they will be arrested." She studied his face for a moment before leaving the room to refill her coffee cup and sit down at the table. A wave of relief flooded over her when he followed and sat down across from her. Maybe he can forgive me, she thought.

"I've just blown my cover with the FBI by telling you all of this. You know, I never thought I'd ever fall in love, but I have. And I don't want to keep anything from you."

"Last night was that part of your FBI cover?"

"Greg, no, what I told you about my brother-in-law is all true." She looked across the table at him. "You are the first man who has ever touched me like that and I'm here because I love you. It has nothing to do with the FBI."

"If you tell Boswell about my involvement with Westmoreland or that I'm working with the FBI, he'll tell others in the department. Next thing you know, everyone will be in on my little secret. If you tell, then you might as well put a bullet through my head because if you don't the crooked cop in the department will."

Greg moved so he was sitting next to her. "But I can't leave Boswell in the dark he's our boss and deserves to know what's happening."

"So do you know who the dirty cop is? Because I don't and I've been trying to find out."

"I can't leave Boswell in the dark. I don't work that way."

She stood, ran a hand down the side of his face and smiled. "I know you and Leroy Allen are going back to Quincy. Agent Ricky Kemp, my contact at the FBI in Atlanta, will be out here while you're away to fill in the chief?"

Greg stood, pulling her into a tight embrace. "Do you have any idea how much I love you?"

Snuggling up against him, she tilted her head to kiss the underside of his chin. "I love you, too."

Chapter Twenty-Four

Bright and early Monday morning, Greg and Leroy met at the airport for the flight to Boston where they rented the cheapest car available and drove the twenty miles to George Cutler's home in Quincy. George met them at the front door, anxious to go to the police station to confront Officer Goodwin. Greg assured him that they would get to it soon, but first he thought they all needed to sit down and have a bit of a chat. George reluctantly agreed and led the two detectives into his still spotless kitchen where he offered fresh coffee and warm bagels both men accepted his generosity and made them selves comfortable at the kitchen table while George busied himself at the counter.

"Thanks, George," Greg said when the other man sat a steaming mug in front of him. "I want to show you something." He opened his briefcase to remove a large manila envelope, which he immediately handed to George.

George accepted the envelope warily, turned it over in his big hands as if he thought the backside might somehow reveal a clue about the contents. When nothing was revealed, he sat down heavily and slowly opened the envelope to spill the contents onto the tabletop. He stared in wide-eyed wonder at the large photo that had ended up on top of a stack of others.

"Is it Beth?"

"That's her," Greg replied.

George shuffled through the photos, stopping to pick up one of his brother with a woman he did not recognize. He looked at it for long moments before turning to Greg with a question in his eyes.

"Her name was Suzanne Akin. That is David standing next to her, isn't it?"

"Yes," George answered as he placed the photo of Beth next to the one of David and Suzanne. "Beth certainly looks like David, doesn't she?"

"Here's a copy of Beth's birth certificate" Greg said pulling it from the stack and holding it out. "Date of birth was March 15, 1977 and David Cutler is listed as her father. She's nineteen months older than Tammy."

He then picked up the three diaries, fanning them in his hand like playing cards. "These are the diaries that Bethany's mother kept—they cover most of her life. She wrote about the day she met David, about how much she loved him, and about their passionate affair. She knew he was engaged to be married to someone else, but it didn't matter to her." Greg handed them to George. "I'll let you read it all for yourself just like I did. When you finish, you'll know what a great person Susan was—she didn't like the name Suzanne and she didn't want to be called Susie or Sue. Apparently, she always introduced herself as Susan."

George ran his hands over the small journals, his voice choked with emotion. "I don't know what to say." He looked up at Greg. "You still have Beth in a safe place, don't you?"

"Don't worry. She's safe."

"I should go down to Georgia to be with her."

Leroy, who had been silent up until now, spoke up. "In time, George, but we have some other work to do first. We need to know who you talked to about the papers you found."

George nodded. "I told my wife, of course. And I talked about it with Tammy when she was here." Overcome by emotion, he closed his eyes and drew a deep breath before continuing. "You know I went to the Quincy police station to look up the homicide report on Benny Trotter. I also wanted to see if I could find some information about David's 'accident' that's when I met Officer Goodwin, who's the only other person I've told, except you people."

"Did Greg tell you that the same gun

that was used to kill Benny Trotter and the Armstrong's was also used to kill Brenda . . . I mean Tammy?"

George shook his head as Greg moved to the coffee maker on the counter and refilled his mug. "I hope when we tell Quincy's Chief of Police what we suspect, he'll let us talk to Goodwin."

"She, not he," George said.

"Huh she who," Greg asked

"The Chief of Police is a she not a he. Her name is Nancy Pitford and she's a good woman but she doesn't like outsiders snooping around her town," George warned.

Greg sipped from his mug, and then smiled at the other two men. "Who's snooping? We're just up here trying to link a murder case in Georgia to one here in Quincy."

Leroy rose from the table with a look of concern on his face. "Hold on, partner. Don't you think we should call in the FBI boys?"

Greg shook his head. "Not yet. We don't know for sure that anyone in Quincy is connected with the murders in Georgia. All we want to do at this point is talk with the Chief of Police. If we find a connection we call in the Feds.

"George, I never did ask how Goodwin was the one who ended up offering to help you with your search."

George shrugged. "He just came up to me and asked if I needed some help. I told him what I wanted and he provided it."

A sudden tingle of apprehension ran down Greg's spine. "Did he ask you anything personal?"

"Like what?"

"Oh, I don't know. Maybe he asked if you and Trotter had been friends or something like that."

"No. But when I told him who I was and explained that I wanted information about the car explosion that killed my brother, he was very helpful."

"What else did he ask you?" Greg pushed for more, thinking there had to be a connection somewhere.

Leroy, who had reseated himself at the table, shook his head in confusion. "I'm not following you, Greg. What are you getting at?"

Greg paced the length of the kitchen. "I'm really not sure, but something keeps gnawing at me. Quincy isn't that small so the police force is probably good-sized. So how did Goodwin just happen to be the one to offer to help George? What are the chances of that being coincidental?

"The other night when Beatrice Langston called me, she mentioned Goodwin said he was a crooked cop, then and now. I'm trying to figure out what part he played in the murders in Georgia?"

"I don't know," George responded. "I remember walking in and looking around for the information desk but before I could get to it, he approached me.

"You know, I didn't even think to look at the signature on the police report. I only looked when you pointed out that Goodwin was the investigating officer."

Greg shrugged. "Don't beat yourself up over it. Even if you had noticed the name no reason for you to make a connection and as far as the police were concerned, the case was closed.

"I hope we're about to blow everything wide open, you boys about ready to stir up some shit?"

Both men nodded and George smiled. "It's about damn time!"

When they left the house, Greg asked George to get behind the wheel of the rented car because he knew his way around town. "George," he asked as the other man backed the car into the street and headed toward town. "Did Goodwin ask you any other personal questions, anything at all?"

George glanced at him in the rear view mirror. "We just talked no, wait a minute.

He did ask if I knew where my niece was and I told him no. I explained that I had hired a private investigator to try to locate her based on the computer-enhanced photo I had I never mentioned a niece. He asked me. The son-of-a-bitch acted so concerned, and all the time he was digging for information about Philip Sharply."

Leroy looked over at George. "You didn't know, man. And hind-sight's twenty-twenty."

"Someone was watching you," Greg said from the backseat. "They knew you'd eventually try to find your niece so all they had to do was to sit back and wait, which is exactly what they did. I wonder why they wanted Sharply dead, though?

"I know he was involved in a big drug operation up here before he disappeared, but they couldn't have been afraid he would talk not after twenty years."

Recalling his recent conversation with Kate, Greg continued, "Sharply embezzled money from them. He took enough to lay low for ten years before he came to Cleveland. But where was he and why did he suddenly reappear?"

Pulling into an empty space in the police station parking lot, George cut the motor and turned to Greg. "What now?" he asked with a quaver in his voice.

Long legs cramped from sitting in the back seat for too long, Greg got out of the car to stretch a bit the other men followed him. "As far as I know," he explained, "Goodwin doesn't know what either Leroy or I look like though at this point, I wouldn't want to bet on it. We'll go in to see if we can meet with the chief.

"George, give us about five minutes and then come in. If we can get in to talk to her, we'll let her know you'll be joining us. Does that sound okay?" They nodded their agreement.

"Then let's go. George, stay cool."

"I'm cool," he said, attempting to smile

it didn't quite work and Greg stopped for a minute to give his shoulder a reassuring pat. George closed his eyes, drew a deep breath, and then nodded at Greg. "I'm cool," he repeated, and this time Greg believed him.

"Good man," he said as he and Leroy turned and crossed the parking lot to enter the building where they waited for several minutes before the officer behind the desk could free himself from his paper work to ask if there was something he could do for them.

Both men presented their badges before Greg spoke. "We'd like to meet with Chief Pitford."

The uniformed officer smiled broadly. "Well, what do we have here, a couple of southern cops on a mission? Let me guess, Alabama, right?"

"Wrong. Georgia. Now, may we see Chief Pitford?" Leroy asked his annoyance at the sergeant's behavior clear in his voice.

"I've often wondered if you boys really eat all that watermelon like I've heard."

"About as much as you boys up here eat clam chowder," Greg retorted as he leaned forward and sniffed the air. "Must be why everything smells so fishy around here." He straightened, giving the man a cold, hard stare. "Now, cut the shit and call your boss."

Chief Pitford, who appeared to be in her mid-forties, wore her black hair in a French twist at the nape of her neck and very little make-up except around her dark eyes, which made them seem overly large in her pale face. She greeted the two men with a smile and a firm handshake as she led them into her office and ushered them to identical fake-leather chairs in front of her desk. Seating herself on the opposite side of the desk, she looked expectantly from one man to the other.

"It must be an important case to bring the two of you all the way up here from Georgia. How can I help?"

Greg told her about the murders

explaining that Armstrong was really Philip Sharply from Quincy. And he told her the gun used to kill the Armstrong's had been used in a murder in Quincy twenty years earlier. Leroy chimed in to let her know Brenda Armstrong, Sharply's adopted daughter, had also been killed with the same gun.

Chief Pitford listened intently while they told their convoluted tale, and then leaned forward, pen poised over a pad of paper so she could take notes. "Do you have a suspect in custody?"

"Not yet," Greg answered.

She leaned forward, looking from one detective to the other. "I don't understand how any of this information will help us solve a twenty-year-old murder."

Greg opened his briefcase to pull out the paperwork relating to Trotter's murder and the car bombing passing them across the desk into her outstretched hand. "We think there might be a problem with the detective who handled the investigation in both of these cases."

She opened her mouth to respond at the same moment that someone knocked softly on the door. "Come in," she called, impatience at the interruption clear in her voice.

George came in and stood uncertainly in the doorway, looking from one detective to the other. Greg stood to greet him. "George, come in, please. Chief Pitford, this is George Cutler his brother was the man killed by the car bomb . . ."

"And, what does he have to do with any of this?"

"If you would take a few minutes to read the reports and review the pictures before I explain, I'd appreciate it," Greg said.

She stared at Greg for a long moment before turning her attention to George. "Fine, sit." She turned her attention to the reports, reading quickly, and then turned to look from one man to another with a shrug of her slender shoulders. "I don't see a problem here. Carl Goodwin is one of our best, but, I'm sure you think you see something, otherwise you wouldn't be here. So, tell me."

Picking up the stack of photographs, Greg lined them up in front of her across the desk. "Well, one thing is that I don't believe so much damage," he pointed at a picture of the car, "could be caused by mechanical failure. If that was true, most of the damage would be under the hood, not in the interior," he said as she leaned forward to study the photos more closely. After a few moments of intense scrutiny, she nodded at Greg. "All right," and then she picked up the phone to buzz the sergeant at the front desk.

"Steve, is Carl working today?" She listened to the response. "When he comes in, have him to report to me. No big hurry, I need his advice on something though."

"Detective Garrison, I've known Carl Goodwin since I came to work for this department at the age of nineteen. I find your insinuations insulting Carl is an honest man who would never be involved in a murder or a cover-up of any kind.

"You're talking about a twenty-year-old crime very few of us would have known the effects of a car bomb back then. Carl may have been mistaken, but to say that it was deliberate is preposterous." She tossed the photos across the desk in his direction.

"Chief Pitman, do you think it was easy to approach you with our suspicions? But, the fact still remains the case should have been investigated further, even twenty years ago." He pulled another envelope from his briefcase and held it out to her. When she refused to take it from his outstretched hand, he tossed it onto her desk. "It's an affidavit that David Cutler signed in front of a Notary Public. You might want to read it.

"Cutler implied that there was a dirty cop working within this department. I'm not saying it's Goodwin, but something is definitely rotten in Denmark and it has his signature all over it."

With a sigh, she opened the envelope, withdrew its contents and began reading. Her pale face turned even paler and her hands trembled visibly as she turned page after page of the document. "My, God," she said at last. Greg nodded and opened his mouth to respond only to be interrupted by a rapping on the door, which was quickly followed by the appearance of a gray-haired office who couldn't be anyone other than Carl Goodwin.

"Nancy? You wanted to see me?" The color drained from his face as he recognized George Cutler, but he maintained his composure as he turned toward his chief with a question in his eyes.

"Come in, Carl. Shut the door, please and pull up a chair." She waited until he was seated before continuing. "Carl, these two men are detectives from Georgia they're investigating a recent string of murders." She didn't offer any explanation for their presence in Quincy and he didn't ask. "This other gentleman is George Cutler, who lives here in town."

Goodwin looked from Greg to Leroy, who stared back at him silently, but he avoided George Cutler's gaze. "What does a murder in Georgia have to do with me?"

Nancy handed him the reports about the Trotter murder and the car bomb, which she had just read. "You were the investigating officer on both of these. I know it's been a long time ago, but take a look what do you remember about them?"

Carl looked at the three men and then down at the sheaf of papers clutched in his hand. He studied them briefly before tossing them onto the desk, looking the chief in the eye. "You're right. It was a long time ago. I can read the reports, but I don't remember anything.

Noticing the way his smile didn't quite

reach his eyes and the way his fingers nervously thrummed on the arm of the chair, Leroy spoke up. "Car explosions must be pretty common around here."

Carl shrugged. "Of course not but come on. Twenty years is a long time, buddy."

Greg grabbed the photos and spread them in front of Carl. "How did you determine this was caused by a mechanical failure?"

Not even bothering to look at them, Carl stared at him. "Like I said, it was a long time ago I don't remember."

Gathering up the photos, Chief Pitford held them out to her officer, who reluctantly took them from her outstretched hand. "Carl, please look at them and try to remember something."

He flipped through the pictures quickly, not really looking at them at all before he shrugged again. "Sorry."

"How well did you know Philip Sharply?" Greg asked, changing his approach in hopes of tripping the officer up. He knows something, he thought. And I want to know what.

"Who?"

"Philip Sharply."

"I don't know anyone by that name."

"That's not the impression you gave Mr. Cutler when he asked your help in locating this," he picked up a sheaf of papers from the desk and waved them at Carl. "The car bomb report."

"The guy looked lost so I asked him if he needed some help that's my job"

"Do you make a point of approaching every lost-looking citizen who walks in or just this one in particular?"

"I was at the desk when he came in."

"Watching for him?" Leroy asked.

Carl jerked around to look at Leroy. "Don't be a chump. Why would I be watching for him?"

"Then, why didn't you explain to him that you were the investigating officer?"

"Why should I? My name's on the report, isn't it?"

George, who had merely sat and listened as the conversations whirled around him, turned to Goodwin with a question. "You asked me if I'd found my niece. How did you know that my brother had a child? And how did you know I was looking for her?"

Greg took out the newspaper clipping about Tammy's adoption and handed it to Chief Pitford before turning back to Goodwin. "You knew Philip Sharply had adopted Tammy Cutler and skipped town it's the only way you could have known that George Cutler didn't know where she was. Am I right?"

Goodwin ignored the question, stood and deliberately turned his back on the three men as he spoke to the chief. "Nancy, do I really have to sit here and listen to this garbage? I can imagine how terrible it must have been for this gentleman to see those people blown to bits like they were pieces of their skulls blown off and all, but it has nothing to do with me."

Chief Pitford stared at him in confusion what in the world was he talking about? Greg knew and held up a cautioning hand to silence her. "Leroy," he asked his voice dangerously soft. "Do you know anything about the way our victims looked when we found them?"

Leroy turned to Goodwin, a smile playing around the corners of his mouth as he shook his head. "No. I have no idea what type of injuries they sustained."

"Officer Goodwin, how do you know?"

Chief Pitford dropped the newspaper clipping on the desk and looked at her long time friend with a mixture of shock and disgust. He knew something. Damn it, he knew.

Beads of sweat popped out on Carl's forehead as he looked from one expectant face to the other. "I read it in the paper."

"No, you didn't. A description of the gunshot wounds was never released. Here's how I see it, Carl. You either committed the murders or you know who did. Now, which is it?"

Carl leaned back in his chair, legs crossed and a genuine smile on his face. "You have no jurisdiction here. I don't have to tell you anything."

"Well, I do have jurisdiction here and you damn well better tell me how you know." Nancy snapped angrily.

Carl stared into her accusatory eyes and felt his heart sink. What had he done? A friendship of more than twenty years had just slipped through his fingers because he was an idiot an old fool who thought he could get away with something he'd had no business messing with in the first place. "What's the use? I'll tell you everything I know. I'm ready to get this mess off my chest anyway."

Heart aching at the loss of her friend and of a man she had always admired as a good officer, Nancy jumped to her feet. "You don't say a word until I get legal in here you won't get off on that defense." She picked up the phone, punched in a number and requested an attorney be sent to her office as soon as possible.

Turning to Leroy with a wink, Greg said, "You might want to place that call to the FBI now. I think we're out of our jurisdiction."

Chapter Twenty-Five

Blissfully unaware of what was transpiring in Quincy, Kate sat in her car in the McDonalds parking lot, sipping on a diet coke. Her radio squawked loudly and as she reached to answer the call, the passenger door open and Officer Daniel Sprayberry got in. "What the hell are you doing?" she asked more in surprise than alarm.

"Don't answer it," he ordered, knocking her hand away from the radio.

She looked at the gun clutched tightly in his right hand first, and then at the man behind it. "Sprayberry of all the possibilities, I'd have never guessed it was you."

Tall and lanky, his knees banged against the dashboard of the Camaro but he didn't seem to notice as he turned to her with a sneer on his lips "Why? Did you think I was too dumb?"

Shaking her head, Kate glanced around the parking lot, hoping to catch sight of another police officer or someone she might signal for help. Other than the few cars she assumed belonged to employees, the lot was empty she and Sprayberry were alone "No," she responded as she looked directly into his eyes. "In fact, I thought you were smarter than that."

He pointed to her ring of keys hanging from the ignition with the gun. "Shut up and start the damn car."

"Where are we going?" she asked nervously.

Jamming the gun into her side hard enough to make her gasp, Sprayberry checked out the immediate area. "Drive out to the main road and turn towards Gainesville. Do it!" he ordered as if she had voiced an objection.

"Okay. I'm doing it, see? No reason to get angry."

Her mind whirled as they rode along in silence. Was there a way to escape or could she manage to get the gun away from him without getting herself hurt? Sprayberry wasn't a big guy not like Greg, but he was a lot bigger than she was. It would be difficult to keep the car under control and struggle with him too. No, she told herself, better to wait for a more opportune moment.

"You murdered the Armstrong's, didn't you?"

He watched the road as she talked. "That piece of shit Armstrong. He was so eager to help me that he never saw the light of day until it was too late."

"But, how did you gain access to the house?" she inquired.

He looked at her in disgust, and then returned his gaze to the road as if he expected her to try to trick him in some way. "I thought detectives were supposed to be smart. If you can't figure that out, you need to go back to school." He glanced at her again. "I waited until I saw the lights come on downstairs I knew someone was up then and I rang the doorbell. As soon as he answered I told him there'd been a jailbreak and the escapee had been spotted at the back of his house."

He threw back his head and laughed as if at a great joke only he knew the punch line to. "The son-of-a-bitch invited me in. He even gave me a cup of coffee before I wondered out into the backyard to look for nothing. As I went back into the house, his old lady came into the kitchen perfect timing. For me anyway," and he laughed again.

Returning to his story, he made a little moue of displeasure and began speaking in a falsetto as he mimicked Bette Armstrong. 'Honey, why are the police here?'" I explained the 'situation' to her, and then told them that everything looked clear and I needed to call in.

"I walked as far as the entryway to the kitchen, pulled the Lugar out, turned and fired—blam, blam, blam! Just like that," there was absolutely no regret in his voice as he recounted the murders and Kate felt a finger of apprehension run up and down her spine as she tried to stay calm.

"And yet you stabbed them too."

He nodded in agreement. "Yeah, I did. Everything was going as planned until that girl came in and scared the shit out of me." He turned to her, a humorless grin spreading across his face. "What the hell, I thought. I just killed two people, one more won't make a bit of difference.

"I stepped back into the shadows of the front room and waited until she walked past, then I sneaked up behind her."

Interrupting his recollections of the murder, he looked at Kate for a moment. "You're taking the girl out of the hospital."

She glanced at him quickly before turning her attention back to the road. "Why do you want Beth? She didn't see anything."

"Is that what she's saying? If she is, she's lying. I was there, remember? I had the knife drawn back," he raised his arm up and back to demonstrate the motion for Kate, "but she heard me and whirled around. We were standing face to face until I grabbed her and spun her around again—I stabbed her in the back and she went down. I think she passed out from fright more than anything else."

He shook his head. "I don't know what happened but I just couldn't bring myself to kill her. Instead, I dragged Armstrong's wife over next to him and then gave both of them a few whacks."

Kate glanced discreetly down at the radio, which still squawked with the sound of the dispatcher's voice as he tried to get Kate to answer. Unfortunately, he didn't sound too alarmed yet, which could be because she wasn't officially on duty right now and he might just think she was away from the car. Keep him talking, she thought. Greg and Boswell will be so pleased when you can provide so many details about the murders.

"There was a lot of blood at the scene. How did you avoid getting it all over yourself? Surely you didn't walk outside covered in the stuff, did you?"

He shook his head. "I spread a few sheets of the newspaper on the floor before I moved Bette Armstrong's body. After I finished the job, I got a trash bag from the cabinet and stepped back onto the newspaper. I stripped naked and put everything, including the newspaper, in the bag. No streaks or splatters from my clothes on the floor and I was very, very careful not to step in anything when I walked out. Westmoreland took the bag up north when he left town."

Attempting to pull her cell phone from her purse without drawing his attention, Kate kept talking. "You walked out of the house naked?"

He pointed the gun at her head. "Put your hand back on the wheel where I can see it or I'll kill you right here."

She glanced at the speedometer. "You'd shoot me while we're going sixty miles an hour? May as well shoot yourself because you'd be dead too."

Leaning across her to grab the purse, Sprayberry momentarily blocked her view of the road. "Hey, move, I can't see," she yelled, grabbing the steering wheel with both hands so she wouldn't lose control of the car.

He pulled her purse free and placed it on the floorboard between his feet. "You must think I'm a real dumb ass!" Then, he remembered the question she'd asked him. "No, I didn't walk out of the house naked. I brought a bag with clean clothes and shoes with me and sat it outside the front door. Armstrong never saw it when he let me in."

"Why did you kill Brenda Armstrong?"

Daniel smirked. "Hell, I thought the girl who walked in on me was Brenda Armstrong. But I was wrong. Brenda was outside and <u>she</u> saw me come out. She went inside and saw what had happened. She must have come running back out and saw me drive past in my police cruiser, and then the idiot followed me. A few days later she called me at the precinct.

"I don't know why she didn't call in the murders and turn me in right then maybe she was in shock or something, but whatever it was worked to my advantage. I knew where she lived in Athens so it was just a matter of time.

"Your lover boy, Greg, was up in Quincy playing detective while you were back here working hard to please him. Stupid Boswell didn't have a clue about what was happening right under his nose."

He shrugged. "So I went to pay little Miss Brenda a visit.. As luck would have it, she wasn't there." He leaned closer to whisper as if he was afraid someone else might be listening in would share in the secret meant for Kate's ears only. "Bet you all didn't know about the houseboat, did you?"

He didn't wait for her response. "So, on a hunch, I made a trip up to Lake Lanier. And sure enough, there she was. Imagine her surprise when I walked in on her in her little hideout. I handcuffed and gagged her and took her back to Athens." He paused for a moment. "And you know the rest of the story," he added with a smile.

She nodded, swallowing hard to tamp down the fear that threatened to engulf her to make her helpless and hopeless, and she couldn't allow that, wouldn't allow it. "You were the one who broke into my apartment, weren't you?"

He studied her for a moment, eyes going dark and hungry at the memory of her naked body writhing under his hands. "So sweet in your bubble bath, so soft . . ." He gave himself a shake not now, he thought. But maybe "I could have killed you then if I'd wanted to. But Westmoreland only paid me to scare you."

She drew in a deep breath. "How much did he pay you to kill the Armstrong's?"

"Fifty thousand."

She smirked. "Well, he was right about one thing country cops can be bought cheap." He made no response, simply stared out the window for a moment as they passed the sign welcoming them to Gainesville.

"You know where we're going so shut up and drive." He jammed the gun into her side again and she winced, but refused to give him the satisfaction of hearing her cry out in pain and fear.

She parked the car in the visitor's parking lot and they walked across the parking lot to enter the Hall Sanitarium. Sprayberry held the gun in his pocket and smiled at her as if they were having a pleasant conversation.

"I've got a full clip in this gun. You do anything to try and warn anyone, and I'll kill you first, and then as many people as I have bullets for," he warned.

Stopping at the front desk, Kate showed her badge and asked for Dr. Hargrove. After a brief phone conversation, the clerk on duty directed them to take the elevator directly to the second floor where the doctor would meet them. As they stepped into the hallway, Dr. Hargrove emerged from his office and smiled in Kate's direction.

"Detective O'Connor," he said as he drew nearer. "What brings you here?"

Kate smiled in return, hoping that it looked genuine she couldn't stand the thought of causing this man, or anyone else here to be hurt or possibly killed. "Greg sent me to pick up Bethany and bring her to police headquarters. We think we've found the killer. We need to see if she can identify him in a line-up."

"She will be so glad to hear that. Where's Detective Garrison now?"

Smiling, Sprayberry stepped closer to Kate. "The suspect's lawyer is at the courthouse trying to get him released. And Greg is . . . meeting with the D.A. Don't worry. He sent me as Kate's backup to make sure your patient stays safe."

Dr. Hargrove quickly wrote out a day pass and handed it to Kate. "I put her check-in time as eight o'clock tonight. Will that be long enough?"

"That will be plenty of time," Sprayberry answered.

Shaking first Kate's hand, and then Sprayberry the doctor promised to have Beth join them in just a few moments. He was as good as his word Beth came hurrying down the hallway to stop in front of Kate. She didn't even glance in Sprayberry's direction as she reached out for one of Kate's hands.

"You're cold," she said, then continued in a breathless rush. "What's happening? Where am I going?" she asked.

Sprayberry pressed the gun harder into Kate's back and she squeezed Beth's hand reassuringly. "I'll explain on the way."

Once outside, Beth took a deep breath and turned her face up to the sun for a moment. It felt so good to be outside in the fresh air again. Kate took hold of her elbow, urging her toward the car. "Why the big hurry, Sergeant? What's going on? Has Detective Garrison caught the murderer?"

Sprayberry opened the front passenger door of Kate's car, took Beth's arm and helped her none-too-gently into the vehicle. "She told you she'd explain on the way," he reminded her as he slammed the door.

"Don't even think about it," he said to Kate, reading her mind. "You make a break for it and I'll shoot you in the back before I put a nice little hole in her head." He nodded toward the car to make sure Kate knew exactly who he was talking about. "Get in," he commanded, opening the rear door. With a sigh, Kate complied, sliding in behind the wheel as Sprayberry clambered into the backseat.

As Kate started the car and began

backing out of the parking space, Beth raised her face and sniffed at the air. "Hold on," she said with an edge of panic in her voice. "I recognize that smell it's the after shave lotion I smelled that morning at the Armstrong's house."

She turned to look at the man in the back seat with horror-filled eyes. "I remember now! It was you! You're the murderer!" she screamed, turning for the door. "Let me out! Let me out!"

Sprayberry swung the gun, cracking Beth on the side of the head. She fell forward and then slumped against the back of the seat—she was out cold.

Kate raised her arm in an attempt to block him, but he was faster than she was and hit the unconscious girl a second time. "Daniel, stop it," Kate pleaded. "You'll kill her."

He snorted derisively, but backed away. "I got news for you. She's dead anyway. Now drive you'll turn when I tell you to turn. Don't even think about speeding either, you got that? I've got a clear view of the speedometer."

Kate watched her speed, turning where she was told to, traveling the back roads on the outskirts of Cleveland until she was ordered back onto Highway 129 where they continued heading north for a few miles.

"Turn left here," Daniel ordered. She slowed and turned Old Corn Stalk Road the old mill, she thought as it came into view. The sweet memory of the day Greg brought her here rushed up to meet her and she had to blink hard to hold back the tears

"Slow down. You just passed it." Daniel yelled and Kate hit the brake, put the car in reverse, and then turned down the dirt path.

She stopped in the overgrown yard and looked over at Beth, who had blood trickling down the side of her face. "Jesus, Daniel, you cracked her head open!"

"Shut up, woman," he practically growled at her. "Get out of the car."

Daniel held his gun on Kate while she tugged and pulled Beth inside the old mill. The walls on the water side had long since decayed and the sight of the water cascading down a steep incline to crash onto the rocks and boulders below would have been breathtaking had it not been for the thunderous roar inside the old structure, which caused the structure to shake making Kate fear for their safety rather than enjoy the view. An impossibility anyway since Daniel was still pointing his gun at her. A large cedar post supported the roof. Most of the boards covering the roof were missing.

"Put her over there against that post," Daniel ordered. Kate turned to eye the cedar post at which he pointed—it, along with one other post, supported what was left of the roof, which wasn't much. She gingerly sat Beth on the ground where the girl moaned in agony, but didn't open her eyes.

Daniel tossed a set of handcuffs to Kate. "Secure her hands around the post."

Being as gentle as possible, Kate positioned Beth next to the post, shifted her so her head and shoulder would rest against it, then pulled her arms around the post and secured them with the handcuffs.

Kate stood and turned to face their captor. "Daniel, you'd better wake up if you think Westmoreland cares about you—he's just using you to do his dirty work."

Daniel was busily ripping strips of duct tape from a roll he'd pulled out of his pocket, but he stopped for a minute to think about Kate's statement. Then he shrugged and went back to work. "That's the difference between men and women, I guess. Women worry about what other people think of them. But give a man enough money and he doesn't care what anyone thinks." He tore off a strip of tape and pressed it around Beth's mouth before pointing to the other post. "Get over there and hug it."

Kate stared at him through wide,

frightened eyes. "Daniel, please don't do
this. Think about your wife and kids. What
will happen to them when you're caught?"

Chapter Twenty-Six

Greg and Leroy waited impatiently in a large conference room with the two FBI agents who had responded to Leroy's call for assistance. Mark Beacham, the older of the two, was dressed nattily in a dark blue suit, crisp white shirt and burgundy and blue striped tie someone must have told him that blue is a good color for him, Greg thought idly as he strummed his fingers on the table top. He could almost hear a woman's voice assuring Beacham that it "brings out the blue of your eyes," and the guy taking the comment to heart.

Beacham's partner, the much younger Frank Desmond, was dressed in much the same way, but somehow it seemed friendly on him more, this is the way they tell me to dress and I do it, but hey, don't let the clothes fool you, man. I'd rather be playing baseball and drinking a few beers with the guys, but it's a job, and a pretty good one at that. Maybe it was the boyish twinkle in his green eyes or the way he kept running his hands through his short red hair and whistling some half-familiar tune under his breath until his partner shot him a look.

Then he'd grow quiet for a few minutes, but it wouldn't be long before he was fidgeting in the chair again. Maybe that's what Greg liked about him the idea that he was ready for action, wanted to get something done rather than simply sitting here waiting. He was like Greg in that respect so he could relate to him much easier than he could to the suit who sat patiently sipping lukewarm coffee from a paper cup as he waited no hurries, no worries there.

It had been well over an hour since George Cutler was sent home under protest and Goodwin had gone into a private meeting with his attorney, who the department's legal counsel had insisted on calling immediately upon being assessed of the on-going situation. And finally, just when Greg thought he couldn't stand the waiting for another minute, Chief Pitford entered the room followed by the sergeant from the front desk, carried a video recorder and a tripod. He busied himself setting up the equipment, and then turned to Greg as if to say something, but changed his mind and left, shutting the door with a little bang. Fifteen minutes later, Goodwin and his lawyer, Jacob Richmond arrived. Show time, Greg thought to himself.

Greg noted with some amusement that Richmond and Beacham were dressed exactly the same even down to the tiepin. He lowered his head and cleared his throat to hold back his laughter when the two men looked each other over angrily, and then studiously chose to ignore one another. Removing his wire-rimmed glasses, Richmond nodded briefly to each person at the table except Beacham, who didn't seem to care.

"I want you all to know that I advised my client against making incriminating statements; however, he has refused that advice and want to discuss everything he knows." He turned to Goodwin. "You're on," he said.

Avoiding Nancy Pitford's unwavering gaze, he cleared his throat, once, twice, and then sipped from a cup he'd carried into the room with him before beginning to speak. "I first got involved with these people back in the mid-fifties. My only child, Carl Junior, had cancer and the medical bills were stacking up. I had no way to pay them. The hospital was threatening to stop treatment if they didn't receive some money. I would've done anything to help my boy." His voice shook with emotion.

"Our friends in the neighborhood and the guys here at the precinct held a fund drive to raise money to help us, which made the local newspapers. Shortly after that, a guy named Gus Steinbeck contacted me, offering me unlimited access to money. All I had to do in return was to tell them when and where the police were planning drug raids. He was my son," he whispered. "So, I agreed.

"They paid off the hospital and doctor bills, which totaled over three hundred thousand dollars and my son received the best care available at the time. I was privy to information within the Narcotics Department so it was easy. I simply placed a call when I had something worthwhile to pass on.

"Carl Junior did fine for a few years at one point he even went into remission. Then, the cancer returned. By the time the doctors found out how bad it was, it was too late. My boy died in 1963 and I tried to break away since I no longer had a reason to work with those people.

"It didn't happen. One evening after I got home from work, another man came to visit me. He said his name was Fidel Marquette I didn't know if that was his real name or not and it didn't much matter. The guy shoved me around, punched me in the stomach and any other place he could think of that wouldn't show when I was dressed. The son-of-a-bitch beat my wife up pretty bad, too.

"I knew then that I'd made a life time commitment whether I'd meant to or not. I wanted to quit the force, but these guys said if I did, my wife and I would be dead they needed my connections here, otherwise I was useless."

He paused, leaning back in his chair and closing his eyes for a moment. "Now, ask me your questions and I'll answer the best I can."

Agent Beacham, who had been sitting half-turned away from the table, whirled around to look Goodwin straight in the eye. "If you wanted out so badly why didn't you go to the FBI? We would have helped you establish another identity under a witness protection plan."

Carl nodded. "I thought about it even discussed it with my wife. But she was a mess. Already torn up over the loss of our son, she couldn't imagine live without the rest of her family around her." He shrugged. "I couldn't do that to her not on top of everything else."

Leroy picked up a police photo and tossed it in front of Carl. "Why did you cover up for the person who killed David Cutler?

Carl stared emotionlessly into the dark eyes glaring back at him. "Detective, when you literally have a gun at your head twenty-four hours a day, you don't ask questions, you do what you're told.

"They knew my district street by street. When Cutler and the woman entered my territory, the remote control was pushed and the bomb detonated end of a problem, or so they thought at the time. I knew it was going to happen and what I was supposed to do." He shrugged again. "I liked being alive so I did it."

Agent Desmond leaned forward in his chair. "Who's your contact man now?"

"Michael Westmoreland."

Greg felt his heart began to do a wild little dance in his chest bingo, he thought. There's our connection. "Who ordered the hit on the Armstrong's?"

"Michael Westmoreland."

"Why?" Greg asked.

"When Philip disappeared twenty years ago, he took millions of dollars of drug money that wasn't his. Someone wanted it back."

"What part did Beatrice Langston play in taking the money?"

Carl smiled and shook his head. "That wasn't her name at the time, but you already know that, don't you? She was Sharply's CPA so they figured she had a hand in it. That's why she disappeared when he did."

"Who murdered the Armstrong's and their daughter Brenda?"

Goodwin looked away from Greg's burning gaze for a moment. "I think you should be worrying more about the new detective working with you."

"Are you talking about Kate O'Connor?"

"That's right."

Greg felt his stomach contract was sure he was about to vomit all over the table and everyone sitting around it. But he took a deep breath, willing himself to stay calm, just stay calm and find out what he's talking about. "Why should I be worried about Kate?"

Ignoring the question, Goodwin stared coldly at Greg. "The person who killed the Armstrong's is one of your police officers."

"What's his name?" Goodwin smiled and Greg lunged for him. Leroy was on his feet, pulling him back into his chair, whispering into his ear. "Be cool, man. Don't buy into his game. Be cool." Pushing him away, Greg nodded. "I'm okay."

A smile spread across Goodwin's face as he looked into Greg's eyes. "It's interesting that I know more about the inner workings of your department than you do, isn't it?" The smile disappeared. "Your officer's name is Daniel Sprayberry."

Greg lunched again, grabbed the old man, pulling him to his feet and shook him like a terrier might shake a rat. "You're a lying son-of-a-bitch!"

Refusing to flinch, Goodwin knocked Greg's hands away and straightened his shirt. "You wanted the truth and that's what I'm giving you. How do you think I know anything about who works for the Cleveland Police Department?"

It's not true, Greg told himself as he moved away from the table. It can't be true. Sprayberry? Why? "How did Daniel Sprayberry get the gun from the Benny Trotter murder?" he demanded.

"When Sharply found out what Trotter was trying to pull, he killed him in a fit of rage. Then he confessed to Westmoreland, who took possession of the gun in question.

"Westmoreland didn't raise a finger to find Philip and Carol he sat back and let David Cutler's brother do all the work. When he found Sharply, Westmoreland sent the gun to Kate O'Connor through a private courier she sent it back.

"Westmoreland told me to take a few days off to visit Cleveland, Georgia. So, I did. I did some snooping and discovered that Sprayberry was up to his eyebrows in gambling debts. The man will place a bet on anything football, baseball, basketball, he even plays the lottery like he's already won. He was on the verge of losing everything."

Carl settled himself more comfortably in his chair and took another sip from his cup before continuing. "So I asked him to meet me one night. I told him I had a proposition he might be interested in. He never flinched when I told him what we needed and how much money he'd get. I came back to Quincy and told Westmoreland we had our man. The rest, as they say, is history."

"Who was the man who accompanied Beatrice Langston to the bank the morning of the murders?" Greg asked.

"Michael Westmoreland."

What a goddamn nightmare this is, Greg thought as he rubbed at the ache behind his temples. "Has Sprayberry been providing Westmoreland with information about our investigation?"

"Constantly."

This guy is one cold mother, Leroy thought with a shiver. He's not confessing out of guilt so what's his motive? "What was Westmoreland's last order to Sprayberry?"

Carl turned to look at Leroy and then back at Greg. "That little girl you think is tucked safely away in the hospital doesn't remember it yet, but she saw Sprayberry inside the house. His order is to kill her along with that pretty new partner of yours.

Remember, no one refuses Michael Westmoreland and lives to tell about it."

Greg stopped dead in his tracks. Bethany Akin was out of harms way at least for the moment, but Kate wasn't. He turned to Chief Pitford, the panic he felt evident in his voice. "A phone," he shouted. "Where's a goddamn phone?"

Nancy jumped to her feet and ran for the door. "Come on. You can use the one in my office."

Hands trembling despite his resolve to remain calm, Greg put in a call to Boswell's private line. "Chief," he yelled, not bothering with formalities. "Where's Kate?"

"Greg? What's up? You almost finished up there?"

"Where's Kate?" he repeated.

Picking up on the panic in the detective's voice, Boswell rose from behind his desk to peer into the outer room. "She's not here she asked for a few hours off this afternoon, said she needed a short breather, and I gave it to her. What's wrong?"

"Is Daniel Sprayberry on the duty roster today?" The ache in his temples was worse and he rubbed furiously at his forehead as he waited for Boswell's response.

"No, he took off today. What do you need Daniel for?" Boswell asked.

"He's our killer. Try to raise Kate on the radio and get her back in there, now!" Greg ordered.

Returning to the conference room with his stomach in knots, Greg started grabbing his papers from the table and stuffing them into his briefcase. Finished, he turned to Leroy. "I need to get to the airport to catch the first flight back to Atlanta." Leroy stood immediately ready to accompany his friend home.

"Hold on a minute, Garrison," Agent Beacham said, also getting to his feet. "Please sit down for a minute."

Hesitating for a moment, Greg turned to study the other man's face, and then nodded.

"Whatever it is, make it quick."

"As quick as possible, three weeks ago, I received a phone call from Beatrice Langston, who told me she had information dating back to the mid-fifties on a number of kingpin drug lords up and down the East Coast.

"I told her to come into the office and we'd talk, but she said it wasn't safe she preferred to remain in hiding. But she did agree to mail copies of some of the information to me so we could verify what she had. Before she hung up, she reeled off a list of names to get our investigation started. It included everyone we've talked about here, plus some. We've been watching these people for years but could never get enough proof against them for an arrest.

"Two days later the package arrived. Our Miss Langston is one shrewd lady. We back-tracked the package starting with the company that delivered it and found she had sent the package from one delivery company to another. When we contacted the original company, we got an address it was a vacant lot in Boston."

He turned to stare down at Goodwin, who appeared to be totally disinterested in the conversation. "In the meantime, Agent Desmond and I dug through the information she sent and yesterday, we took the information to a federal judge who issued an arrest for Michael Westmoreland and several others including you, Officer Goodwin. This morning, our agents arrived at Westmoreland's hideout and surprised everyone inside.

"When our agents burst in, Westmoreland was standing in the middle of the room with a forty-five in his mouth. He pulled the trigger ka-boom! He blew off the top of his own head.

"As of this morning, our agents have arrested over forty major drug dealers up and down the eastern seaboard. All thanks to Beatrice Langston."

Mumbling to himself, Carl refused to meet the agent's gaze. "He who lives by the sword shall die by the sword."

Leroy grunted in disgust. "So, rather than be arrested, chicken shit Westmoreland killed himself."

Beacham nodded, "in front of a room full of federal agents."

"Great news, guys," Greg said as he stood up again. "But I've got to get home now."

Beacham stopped him a second time. "We'll fly you and Leroy back to Atlanta on our private jet. I've already notified Ricky Kemp in our Atlanta branch I'm sure you know he's the agent Kate O'Connor's been working with. He'll have a helicopter waiting to fly you on to Cleveland."

"We left our cars at the airport," Leroy reminded Greg as they stepped into the hallway."

Desmond, who had followed them out, spoke up. "Not a problem. There will be two agents waiting for you in Atlanta. Give them your keys and they'll drive the cars to Cleveland."

"Thanks," Greg said as he patted the agent's shoulder. "You're a good guy. Beacham," he nodded at the other federal agent. "Thanks. Chief Pitman, I'm sorry for your trouble, but thank you for your help. Goodwin it's been real. Send me a postcard from prison, huh?" And with that he was gone, Leroy following in his wake.

The sergeant at the front desk stepped forward to meet them as they approached. "Lieutenant Garrison, could you hold up a minute?"

"What do you want now, Sergeant?"

"I just wanted to tell you and Detective Allen that I'm sorry for the comment I made when you first came in. I was out of line. I sure hope everything works out okay in Georgia." He extended his hand and first Greg and then Leroy shook it heartily.

"Thank you, Sergeant Perkins. And yes,

we do love our watermelons," Greg said smiling.

"And, our soul food," Leroy added.

As they raced toward the airport in the rented car, Leroy filled Greg in on what had transpired while he was on the phone with Boswell. "Nancy told us that Goodwin's wife passed away about six months ago of a heart attack."

Greg shook his head in disbelief, "so much for his excuse of not going to the FBI. What was he waiting for? He never had any intentions of doing the right thing."

Chapter Twenty-Seven

Wide-eyed with fear, Kate leaned her forehead against the cedar post for a moment before turning to look at Beth, who was still unconscious. Daniel had left them here alone about an hour ago, giving no indication as to when he might return if he would return.

Desperate to escape, she attempted to jerk her hands free of the cuffs, but stopped when the unyielding metal tore at her tender skin. Trying to open her mouth behind the strip of tape only resulted in a sore jaw and the roar of the water outside was making her head ache. If only Greg was in town, she thought. He might be able to figure out where we are but he's in Quincy. Their only hope was that someone would start worrying when she didn't return to the station or answer her radio and start looking for her. Maybe they'd do it before it was too late.

From the corner of her eye, she saw movement in the bushes along the water's edge and turned her head in that direction. This was bear country, she thought as her heart began to pound madly in her chest. God have mercy please don't let us become some hungry animal's next meal. When a doe with a fawn close at her side stepped into the clearing, she let out her breath with a great sob. The doe lifted her head for a moment, seeming to stare directly into Kate's eyes, and then turned to bound into the underbrush with her baby close behind Kate caught a flash of their white, bobbing tails before they disappeared from sight.

Tears of relief coursed down her cheeks and she did her best to wipe them away on the shoulders of her blouse. Don't lose it now, Kate. Not now. A plume of dust alerted her to the approach of a vehicle rescue, she thought. Rescue, but I need to scream to let them know we're here. In desperation, she began to rub her face back and forth across her damp shoulder, finally loosing a corner of the tape. She kept rubbing until, miraculously, her mouth was free.

"Help! Help me!" she screamed at the top of her lungs. "I'm in here! Somebody, help me!" When her cries elicited no response, she gave up and began to sob in frustration. A shadow fell across her and she turned quickly to see a tall figure standing in the doorway. "Thank you, God," she whispered before crying out again. "In here, please help me!" The figure rushed forward and her hope disappeared.

It was Daniel. "Shut your fucking mouth," he snarled against her ear. "Who in the hell do you think is going to hear you out here in the middle of nowhere?"

He grabbed the roll of duct tape from the floor where he'd discarded it earlier and ripped off a long strip. Beginning at one side of Kate's mouth, he wound it tightly around her head, and then pressed it firmly in place, not caring if he hurt her perhaps enjoying the thought of causing her pain.

"Let's see you tear that off." And he threw back his head and laughed as if he'd just said the funniest thing imaginable.

"Come on, Kate. You didn't really think I was planning to just leave you here handcuffed to a post did you?" Wide-eyed, she shook her head and watched as he seated himself next to her on the dirty floor, placing her cell phone within arms reach. Then he pulled the portable radio from his belt, turned the volume up as loudly as possible, and pressed it against the side of Kate's face. "Here's a message for you."

Chief Boswell's voice filled her head and she felt another surge of hope as she listened to his words. "Kate, this is Chief Boswell. If you can hear me, please return to the station. Please."

Laughing, Daniel pulled the radio away and turned it off. "Yeah, sure she will." He grew silent for a moment as he stared into Kate's eyes, and then he began to ramble. "By now your sweetie, Detective Greg Alvin

Garrison I'm pretty sure is on his way back to Georgia. Before long, we'll turn on the radio again to hear him begging me to give myself up."

Almost unconsciously, he pulled the German Lugar from his belt, removed the clip to examine it carefully, and then shoved it back into the gun. "I've already killed three people and I've been paid to kill two more," he said, staring into Kate's tear-filled eyes. "But, I'm taking Greg Garrison out free of charge.

"Of course, lover-boy doesn't know I have Miss nosy ass Beth he may not even know yet that I have you. But, he will before the night is over. And once he does, I'll put the fourth and final phase of my plan into action."

He winked at Kate, who only stared back at him. "Oh, I forgot! You don't know what the final plan is, do you?" His smile faded into nothingness. "Don't worry. When the time comes, you'll know everyone will know."

Shaking her head, Kate tried to talk behind the tape, but it was impossible. She raised her head to look skyward as she felt more than heard the thump-thump of an approaching chopper. Maybe they were already searching with a little luck, they'd spot her car and come in for a closer look.

But once more Daniel seemed to read her mind and his words once more sent her hope plummeting into darkness. "They won't see it, Kate. I pulled it into the undergrowth and covered it with a camouflaged tarp." He glanced up as the sound of the helicopter faded into the distance. "See?" he asked with a shrug. Damn it, Kate thought as fear and exhaustion overtook her. She leaned against the cedar post as the hot tears began to run down her cheeks this time, she didn't even try to wipe them away.

Chapter Twenty-Eight

As soon as the chopper touched down in an empty lot behind the police station, Greg was out and running low to avoid the whirling blades. Leroy was at his side and Ricky Kemp, the federal agent who'd joined them in Atlanta was close behind when Boswell flung open the back door of the station to usher them inside.

"Kate?" he asked with no preliminaries.

Boswell shook his head. "Not yet. We've been trying all afternoon, but so far nothing. We can't find her."

They stopped at the dispatch desk and Greg reached across the operator to pick up the mike. "Kate, this is Greg. Please talk to me." There was no response to his plea and he patted the operator's shoulder before replacing the mike and turning away. "What about Sprayberry?"

"I sent a couple of guys out to his house and they talked to his wife she hasn't seen him since early this morning."

Greg's cell phone began to jangle and he grabbed for it, the hope on his face almost too painful for the other men to look at. "Hello."

"Greg?"

His heart leapt at the sound of her voice. "Kate, where are you?"

"You have to listen to me, Greg."

"Honey, are you okay?"

She began to cry softly and he felt the anger rising in his chest. "I'm just frightened, but Beth's been hurt pretty badly," she whispered.

"Beth is with you?"

"Yes."

"Is Daniel there too?"

"Yes. I'm handcuffed and he's holding the phone so I can talk to you. He's not giving me much time so you have to listen."

There was so much he wanted to say needed to say. I love you, Kate, he thought as he nodded. It will all be over soon and you'll be safe in my arms. "I'm listening."

There was the rustle of paper on the other end, and then Kate spoke again. "I'm going to read exactly what he's written.

"Meet me at the old gristmill on Corn Stalk Road. Come alone. If I hear a siren or catch a glimpse of a blue light, both of the women die. If I don't get what I want, they die. If you try to arrest me, they die. When all of my demands have been met, I will set them free." She paused. "That's it. Do you understand, Greg?"

The throbbing behind his temples was back, only this time it felt like a herd of wild horses were stampeding in there. He ignored the pain the best he could Kate and Beth needed him right now. "I understand. Don't worry, Kate. I'm coming." The only response was the buzzing of the dial tone in his ear.

"What did she say?" Boswell questioned.

Greg held up a finger, asking him to wait a minute as he turned to address Ricky Kemp. "Mr. Kemp, I think I need that help you offered earlier."

The four men trooped into Boswell's office where Greg filled them in. Kemp turned to draw the blinds over the windows before placing his briefcase on the desk and withdrawing a tiny microphone, which he attached to Greg's collar the wire leading to the transmitter was no bigger than a couple of strands of hair, making it almost invisible to the naked eye. Next, Kemp pulled out a miniscule earpiece, which Greg placed in his ear as another tiny wire was draped behind his neck, down his back, and into the transmitter, which was clipped inside the waistband of Greg's pants. Kemp ran a few quick tests the equipment worked beautifully.

"We'll be able to hear everything that's being said and you'll be able to hear us." He stepped closer to Greg, pointing at the earpiece. "Whatever you do, do not play

with the earpiece that would be a dead
giveaway to the guy. If he's got any
intelligence at all, he'd figure out that you're
wired and we'd have a big problem. So make
sure it's comfortable and then leave it
alone."

Greg opened his mouth to voice his
fears but Kemp raised his hand. "Don't
worry. You won't even know we're around
until the time is right. And then when I tell
you to do something, you do it!"

Chapter Twenty-Nine

Forty-five minutes later, Greg drove into the clearing in front of the old mill. Caution is the key, he thought as he stepped from the car and took several steps toward the building.

"You looking for us?" a voice behind him called and he whirled to see Daniel walking from behind the sheltering trees. Kate his Kate, was handcuffed and gagged. She stumbled along in front of her captor, who held on to a handful of her dark hair to ensure that she wouldn't try to run. Let's take him down now, Greg thought as he strained to hear the order in the earpiece there was nothing but silence.

"Let her go, Sprayberry," he pleaded.

Daniel pulled the gun from his waistband with his free hand and placed it against the side of Kate's head. Greg saw her wince, but he knew he had to ignore it and concentrate on Sprayberry if he wanted to help her. "Since when did you become top dog? Toss your piece in the water, Garrison."

He shoved Kate, who stumbled and would have fallen had it not been for the hand entangled in her hair that jerked her upward. He jammed the gun against the side of her head again. "Don't try to be a hero, big guy. Do it now or I'll put a bullet through her brain."

Greg reluctantly unsnapped his holster, pulled the gun free and tossed it toward the water. It landed somewhere on the other side of the rock wall with an audible thump. "What now?"

Another shove sent Kate sprawling. She lay still for a moment before finally managing to struggle to her knees in spite of the handcuffs. Greg instinctively began to move forward, but the click as Sprayberry cocked his gun gave him pause, and he stopped in his tracks. For a third time, the barrel of the gun was against Kate's head and Greg watched in helpless anger as she gave in to the tears.

"Not so fast, bad boy," Daniel said, laughing at his own private joke.

Greg looked into Kate's pain-filled eyes for a moment and saw the plea for help there. Hard as it was to do, he looked away. "Why are you doing this, Daniel?"

"I'm getting paid very well, Garrison."

"Yeah, who's shelling out the money? Westmoreland?"

"Well, well, well. Looks like our small town boy might become a pretty good detective after all." Daniel nodded. "Yes. Westmoreland is a very generous man."

Greg laughed, shaking his head. "I don't think you've heard the good news about Westmoreland."

Angered by the other man's laughter, Daniel pointed the gun at him. "Don't try to mind fuck me by saying Westmoreland was arrested. He's too smart for that."

"No. He wasn't arrested. He's dead."

Daniel grabbed Kate and yanked her against his chest. "Bullshit," he screamed. "I'd have to be pretty damn stupid to fall for that."

Greg felt the tall grass crunching under his feet as he began to move slowly toward the wall, all the while keeping his eye on Daniel's trigger finger. Kate watched him for a moment, and then, not able to stand the suspense, turned her attention to Daniel, who didn't seem to notice Greg's movements.

"Dan," Greg said softly. "We've known each other all of our lives. When have you ever known me to bullshit about death?" The other man made no reply, he simply watched as Greg edged ever closer to the wall and his gun. "I just got back from Quincy where I had myself a nice, long talk with Carl Goodwin. You remember Carl, don't you? He told me all about the gambling debts you owe."

He stopped moving as he stared directly into Daniel's eyes. "He's in the hands of federal agents but before they took him away, he fingered you as Westmoreland's hit man. It's all over Daniel. You've got no place to run."

Daniel aimed calmly at Greg's head. "Just in case you have on a bullet proof vest," he explained in a conversational tone. "By the way, I don't need to run to Westmoreland or anyone else. I have enough money to live anywhere in the world. It's been real nice talking with you, Greg."

Kate tried to scream from behind the tape, but no one could hear her. Greg watched as she lunged forward, throwing herself between Greg and the gun.

Daniel stumbled as she pulled from his grasp, pulled the trigger, and stepped back as Kate turned toward him spraying the front of his shirt and face with blood, so much blood. The shock, pain and confusion were clear in her dark eyes as she stared at him for a moment before falling away from him and over the wall. He saw her tumble head over heels once, twice, and then there was a splash as her body hit the water where she lay, face down and unmoving.

Greg watched in helpless horror as Kate took the bullet meant for him. As if from a great distance, he heard himself screaming her name as he lunged forward. He was aware of Daniel's movements saw him raise the gun and cock the trigger, and he stopped in his tracks. I'm dead, he thought as Daniel began to speak. "I'm not even getting paid to kill you." He stepped closer "I don't want to miss," he explained.

Half in shock by what he had just witnessed, Greg watched with disinterest as Daniel's finger started to squeeze the trigger. Boom! Instinct told him to drop, and he did, grabbing his head, feeling for the blood that must surely be flowing from a fatal wound. He glanced back at Daniel who dropped to his knees in slow motion before pitching face down on the ground.

Clambering to his feet, Greg spun around to see a uniformed officer from the White County Sheriff's Department standing behind him with a smoking 30-06 still nestled against his shoulder.

Greg turned and vaulted over the wall. He stumbled and fell, cutting his hands upon the sharp rocks but he was back on his feet and moving again, the blood on his palms unnoticed as he slid the last few feet to gather Kate into his arms. He fumbled in his pocket for his handcuff key, dropping it twice in the mud before finally managing to unshackle her hands. Turning her gently, he removed the tape from around her face and kissed her lips. She's breathing he thought she's still alive. He heard her gasp, felt her fingers on his cheek and turned to stare into her dying eyes.

Unaware of the tears coursing down his face, he brushed the hair from her face and held her tighter against his chest. "Don't you die, Kate," he sobbed. "Don't do it. Hang on. Do you hear me?" There's so much blood, he thought as he placed a hand over the wound in her chest. If I can just stop the bleeding she'll be okay. "Hang on, Kate," he pleaded again, and then he saw her smile.

"No one," she whispered around the blood bubbling slowly from between her lips. "No one has ever been loved—as much as I—by you." She tried to draw a breath, tried to hold on a little longer, but she couldn't. Her eyelids fluttered, her hand slipped from his cheek, leaving a trail of blood in its wake—and she was gone.

Unaware of the sudden activity around him, Greg hugged her lifeless body to his, soaking his clothes with her blood. He looked up to see Boswell and Kemp hovering over him, holding back the press of officers who wanted to move forward to offer comfort to a fellow officer in pain. "Where were you?" Greg screamed at Kemp. "You were supposed to be right behind me." His eyes met Boswell's. "Damn you," he whispered. "Where were you?" He turned his attention back to Kate, who was still dead—still gone.

Boswell knelt at his side, unashamed of the tears running down his face. "It's my fault Greg. I couldn't find the road—couldn't remember where it was. And then we heard the gunshot . . . Oh, God, I'm sorry!" Lost in his own agony, Greg did not respond.

Gun drawn, Kemp stood behind Greg. At his signal, a group of men entered the old building where they found the still unconscious Beth. An ambulance was summoned—the driver had no trouble finding the road, and within fifteen minutes of her discovery, Beth was on her way to Northeast Georgia Medical Center where the prognosis for full physical recovery was good—her mental state; however, was questionable at best.

First Boswell and then Kemp moved away as Greg continued to cradle Kate in his arms, whispered softly into her ear, promising to keep her safe if she'd just open her eyes and look at him. "Open your eyes, Kate", he begged softly even though he knew she would never look at him again. He raised his head when someone touched his arm. Paul Nesbit the State Examiner knelt at his side—sympathy and determination clear in his eyes.

"Greg, you need to let me take her now."

"No, Paul. Not her. You can't have her."

"Greg," he explained patiently. "Kate's gone. You have to let me take the body now. Come on, son. Let me have her." He removed Greg's arms from around Kate and helped him to his feet. He put his arm across the younger man's shoulders and turned him away as his assistants came forward to carry her away.

Greg shook his head before looking into his friend's eyes. "I couldn't save her, Paul. I couldn't save her."

"I know, Greg, I know. Come on, I want you to go to the hospital so they can check you over." Greg opened his mouth to protest—to tell Paul that he was suffering from a broken heart and there were no drugs that could heal it, but Paul held up a hand to silence him. "Uh huh, I've heard it all. Do it for me, Greg." And he did.

The admitting doctor found no physical injuries but ordered a sedative and kept him in a room overnight sometimes, he thought as he injected the drug into Greg's arm, a good night's sleep is the perfect way to start the healing.

Chief Boswell made the painful trip to Athens to give Kate's parents the sad news. As the tears rolled down her mother's face and her father raised a hand to cover his eyes, he told them that she had given her life to save the life of a fellow officer and explained her work with the FBI and told them that Katherine—Kate to her friends and coworkers, O'Connor was a woman of distinguished valor. They should be proud of their daughter. If that's true, he thought as he drove away, then why does my heart feel as if it's being ripped from my chest? Why does the loss of Kate hurt so much?

Chapter Thirty

Two days later, Greg stood amidst a sea of blue uniforms all with black ribbons across their badges, and watched as the body of the woman he loved was lowered into the cold, dark ground. His tears flowed freely—but he knew he wasn't alone in mourning her loss. How am I supposed to say goodbye, he wondered as he stepped forward to drop a handful of dirt onto the casket? How can I let go when I love her so much?

That evening he sat in his den as the ghost of Kate flitted around the room. He saw her everywhere he turned—heard her laughter echoing from every corner. He remembered the sound of her laugh and saw her dark eyes staring trustingly into his as he made love to her for the first and only time. Although they hadn't been together long enough for him to store up a plethora of memories, he knew he would cherish the few that he had—that they would see him through the dark days which surely lay ahead.

He took a month off of work—a month in which he tried to lay Kate's ghost to rest, and then told himself it would have to be good enough—he'd done what he could on his own and work would help heal his wounds in a way that solitude never could. He was ready to get back into the thick of things, to catch up on paperwork and whatever else needed done, but he couldn't concentrate because his gaze kept wondering to the now empty desk where Kate had sat in the not so distant past.

Hearing a commotion in the hallway, he stood just as four uniformed officers entered the room pushing hand trucks loaded with boxes upon boxes. "What the hell is all this?" he asked.

"The information I promised you," he heard a woman say as she entered the room. "As I live and breathe, it's Beatrice Langston." He sat down again.

She strolled across the room to sit in the chair next to his desk. "That's thirty-five years of information on judges, lawyers, bankers, businessmen and politicians. I promised you I'd bring this stuff to you, and here it is."

He smiled at the woman whose life Kate had helped save, "it all belongs to the FBI now."

She shrugged. "Then you give it to them."

She leaned forward to look into his eyes. "I was young and very naïve when I first went to work for Philip Sharply. By the time I figured out what he was doing, it was too late." She leaned back, motioning toward the boxes with a slender hand. "So I started gathering evidence and making copies of everything I could get my hands on.

"I didn't help Philip Sharply take money from anyone my hands never touched it. He did all that on his own. I just took care of the paper work you'll find copies of all of it in those boxes."

"What will happen to you now?"

She sighed. "I plan to testify for the FBI should it ever get to trial. They'll set me up with a new identity and I will disappear into obscurity. Beth has her Uncle George with her hopefully that will help her recovery. God, I wish Tammy was here with them.

"I've already spoke with Agent Beacham and he knows I brought this stuff to you. He also knows where I'll be living in the meantime so I'm not hiding from anyone." She extended her hand to Greg and he took it between both of his. "Detective, I want you to know how grateful I am to you for not giving up on this case. And I am so sorry about Kate. You loved her very much, didn't you?"

"Yes," he whispered. "I do…did." She stood and he stood with her, still holding onto her hand. "Where are you going now?"

She studied his face for a long moment before responding, "back to where I've been all this time to wait for, Agent Beacham to call me. But first, I'm going to see Beth at the hospital. You take care of yourself, Detective."

She stopped at the boxes, rubbing her hand across the top of one. "My whole life is in these boxes what a waste, a terrible waste." She turned to face Greg one final time. "Greg, if you let it, love will find you again." She turned without another word and left the building he never saw her again.

Several more weeks passed and Greg felt the ache around his heart beginning to ease a bit, though his thoughts often turned to Kate. He had the Armstrong case folder spread open on his desk, but wasn't reading anything. Grateful for the distraction provided by ringing phone, he answered it on the first ring.

"Hello."

"Detective Garrison?" a soft, feminine voice asked.

Greg closed the folder, half-listening to the woman on the other end as he stamped the cover of the folder, 'CLOSED' and laid it to one side. "Speaking."

There was a slight pause on the other end. "This is Diane Helton. You may not remember me. We spoke when Brenda Armstrong's body was discovered on the campus of the University of Georgia."

Greg let his mind wander back for a moment remembered Kate as she stood at the bottom of the hill staring up at him as he spoke to the other woman. "Yes, I remember. What can I do for you?"

"I read in the newspaper about your partner's death the article said you two were in love." She paused for a moment. "I've lost someone I loved dearly too. I want you to know that I can relate to your pain."

Greg leaned back in his chair as he tossed his pen onto the desk. "You've had someone you loved shot dead in front of your eyes?" My God, he thought. What are you doing? "I'm sorry," he said before she had a chance to respond. "I didn't mean to sound so harsh."

"That's all right. Believe me, I really do understand. No, he wasn't shot. But Lieutenant, when someone you love is taken from you without any warning, it still hurts."

"Of course it does. I'm sorry. Who are you talking about?"

"My husband."

"How did he die?"

"Remember the plane that blew up in mid air off the coast of New York a few years ago?"

Greg nodded, remembering the pictures of the burning wreckage on television. "Yes, I remember, it was terrible. Was he a passenger?"

He heard her draw a jagged breath before she responded. "Yes, but I never talk about it. I suppose it is my way of dealing with his death. In my mind, he's simply still away on his trip," her voice trailed off.

He dug his fingers into his eyes, hoping to stop the tears that threatened to overflow. "I'm truly sorry, Professor Helton. But, why did you call me?"

"We were only married eleven months when he died they never found his body so I buried an empty casket." She began to sob uncontrollably and Greg sat quietly as he waited for her to regain her composure. "Identifying Brenda's body and then seeing you on television at Ms. O'Connor's funeral finally made me realize that he's not ever coming home. I know it's time to deal with his death," her voice trailed off into a whisper.

Greg wanted to offer words of comfort but his own pain wouldn't let him. "Did he travel for his job?"

"No. He was an architectural engineer isn't it strange how fate can step in and change a person's life forever?"

"I'm sorry. I don't understand what you

mean."

She sighed and then continued, "He wasn't supposed to be on that flight. It was a last minute change of plans. His sister and his niece were booked on that flight to Paris. A few days before they were supposed to leave, his sister had a heart attack—not a serious one, but bad enough that the doctors refused to allow her to go. She called Harvey that was my husband's name, and asked him to go in her place."

She laughed at the memory. "He was so excited. He'd always wanted to see Paris, so he jumped at the offer. Everything was paid for. She even changed the traveler's checks over to his name. All he had to do was pack his clothes and fly to New York."

Her voice became somber again. "So he arranged things at his job, packed his clothes and I took him to the Atlanta airport. We kissed goodbye and I watched him leave. That was the last time I ever saw him."

"I am so sorry."

"Lieutenant, as painful as it may be, life goes on. It's not easy and no matter how hard we try to make sense of it, nothing will bring them back to us."

Afraid to speak, Greg nodded, and then realized that she couldn't see him. "I know," he said through his own tears.

She cleared her throat and sniffed. "I hope you don't think I'm being terribly forward when I say I think we can help each other get past the grief."

"I'm not sure I understand what you mean."

"If I were to invite you over for dinner one night would you come?"

Greg tried to remember what she looked like, but couldn't—it doesn't matter, he thought. It's just dinner. "Sure."

"I'm free tomorrow night if you are."

Greg wrote Kate over and over on a notepad while listening to Diane. "I've got nothing planned." She gave him directions and he promised to be there around seven-thirty.

He left home early enough the following afternoon to drive to Athens and place fresh flowers in the vase on Kate's grave. "I miss you," he whispered as he brushed a few dead leaves from the grave stone. He stood for a long time thinking of what could have been, of what he had hopped would have been. Greg came to the realization that nothing he had wanted would ever come to pass with this woman whom he loved so dearly. He took his cell phone from his pocked and dialed the number Diane had given him.

"Diane, Greg here. I really can't do this. I'm sorry I made this date with you but I simply can't go through with it. Please forgive me."

After a brief silence, Diane spoke. "I do understand what you are going through and I really do wish you would reconsider."

"I'm sorry, but I can't. I hope you have a wonderful life and find love and happiness. Good-bye." He closed the phone before she had a chance to say anything else.

While he stood at the foot of Kate's grave he remembered what Beatrice Langston told him. "Greg if you let it, love will find you again."

"God, I sure hope so," he got in his car and drove home.

(Book one in the Garrison series)

12505279R00124

Made in the USA
Charleston, SC
09 May 2012